Also by Ven Begamudré

THE TELLER
FROM THE TALE

The Teller
From The Tale

Ven Begamudré

Cover art: Nina Paley
Book and cover design: Tania Wolk, Third Wolf Studio
Printed and bound in Canada at Friesens, Altona, MB

The publisher gratefully acknowledges the support of
Creative Saskatchewan and Canada Council for the Arts.

Library and Archives Canada Cataloguing in Publication

Title: The teller from the tale / Ven Begamudré.
Names: Begamudré, Ven, 1956- author.
Description: Short stories.
Identifiers: Canadiana (print) 2020020050X | Canadiana (ebook) 20200201190 |
ISBN 9781989274248
(softcover) | ISBN 9781989274279 (PDF)
Classification: LCC PS8553.E342 T45 2020 | DDC C813/.54—dc23

radiant press

Box 33128 Cathedral PO
Regina, SK S4T 7X2
info@radiantpress.ca
www.radiantpress.ca

for Edna Alford

CONTENTS

AMAR'S GIFT

1

Precious Creations

AMAR LIVED IN A VILLAGE on the shore of Moon Lake in the shadow of Fire Mountain. He was a gentle, young man. While his brothers worked ankle-deep in water or mud in hot sun or pouring rain, he sat in the shelter of their widowed mother's house and carved. But what he carved: shaped by his down-light fingers, a block of wood became a hummingbird, a stone became a rose, a grain of rice a snowflake. At sunset his brothers returned from their paddies and argued over which of them had worked hardest. When they reached their mother's house, they stopped under the eaves to examine Amar's work. They forgot their aching arms and stiff legs while marvelling at his skill though they otherwise cared little for him. The longer they marvelled, the lighter he felt. He thought he could spread his arms and let the wind carry him from people who did nothing but work and eat and sleep and knew of nothing except birth and life and death. When the brothers saw his wistful smile, they frowned. One of them always said, "Ho, Stay-at-Home, you've wasted another day. How many prayers will that flower (or bird or tree) buy for our dead father? When will you set aside your fine clothes and work beside us in your loincloth?"

"Good question," my wife says. "You're supposed to be fixing the upstairs toilet and here you are, spinning stories."

.

"Someone has to," I tell her. "Where would the world be without—?"

"Sweetie," she says, "that same someone promised to spend the first week of his holidays doing chores. Can't the story wait?"

"Fixing toilets reminds me too much of work," I say. "There's only so many times you can rewrite a cabinet document before it starts sounding like fiction."

When she says, "Don't make me laugh," I change the subject.

"So, what do you think of that opening?" Before she can reply, I admit, "It's not the original opening. This was."

We have changed the names but the land remains, and Fire Mountain rises as majestically as ever in what our fathers called the Kingdom of the Sun. Not once in our memories has the mountain erupted, but the last time its flames scorched the sky, it vented enough anger to topple the finest house in the kingdom. The mountain spirits rest now, weakened by their outpouring of rage, but they do not sleep. They only wait for us to forget the value of Amar's gift.

"That's terrible," she says. "It's so…la-de-dah."

I sit there smarting but she's right, as usual, and so I say, "I suppose that's why my editor suggested I drop it. Later on, I realized I was simply writing my way into the story."

"It also gives away too much," she says. She's full of surprises—my wife. Her hair even changes colour according to her moods. This morning she awoke a strawberry blonde. "Way too much," she adds.

"Do you know this story?" I ask.

"I know you," she says.

The day's too young to get into that, so I mutter, "Where was I?"

"The brothers are wondering when Amar will start making himself useful."

At this, he returned to earth. He felt clumsy and homely and chided himself for thinking his works could be any more than curiosities to such practical men. At first he answered, "I cannot work like you with heavy tools." Then he said, "I do what I must." *My wife snorts.*

Over the years the brothers married and built their own houses. Lost in his carving, Amar never returned the teasing smiles of the village women, and so they laughed about him when they gathered at the well.

"He'll search for stones while his children starve," one woman said.

"Better to marry a merchant with fingers soiled by money," said another, "than a craftsman with no ambition."

At last his mother lost her patience. She scolded him in public. "What has all this carving done except heap slivers and splinters under my eaves? Has it raised one stalk of rice or helped your brothers pay my taxes? The house is so full of your precious creations, there's barely room for us to sleep. Should we hang from the rafters like bats?"

The crowd gathering in the street laughed.

Shame reddened Amar's face. He snatched up his tools and a roughly hewn block of wood. But before he could retreat into the house, a stranger stepped from the crowd.

"What precious creations?" he scoffed. "What can there be of value in this sorry village? I'm from Makura. My name is Tambunan. Let me see."

"How dare you call our village sorry?" the innkeeper asked. "Don't we have the finest view in the kingdom of Fire Mountain?"

"Clearly a merchant," the water bearer growled. "Look at his huge belly and twitching fingers!"

"He's no better than an untouchable," the scribe muttered.

"Untouchables bury us when we die. Merchants skin us alive."

Unlike her neighbours, Amar's mother revered anyone who lived in a town. "Lord Tambunan," she said, "I was only jesting about my son's work. It's not really precious. You see, when he's not wandering the slopes of Fire Mountain or the shores of Moon Lake, he carves and polishes worthless curios. Please, see for yourself." She bowed Tambunan into the house and began to make tea.

"How typical!" my wife exclaims. "The men are merchants or water bearers or scribes and the mother makes tea."

"It's that kind of story," I say. "It's set a long time ago—"

"—in a galaxy far, far away?"

"No-o. It used to be set in medieval Japan but I changed it so it's set in Southeast Asia. Somewhere. Indonesia maybe?"

Frowning, she asks, "Aren't you the one who says the more specific a story is, the more universal it will feel?"

"That's true, but my mentor didn't think this felt like a Japanese story, so he suggested I change the setting. Amar's name used to be Kobayashi."

She says, "Your editor, your mentor—whose story is this, anyway?"

"You ask. I answer."

"I prefer Amar," she says. "Where's that from?"

"I asked my mother for some Indian names, and I liked Amar. She suggested Tambunan for the merchant. I think it's Indonesian. But here's the best part. After I told this story in a school, one of the Indian girls said Amar means 'deathless.'"

"You're still giving things away," my wife says. Then, "Wait a minute. You told this entire story in a school and they sat still for it?"

"I told one part every Friday afternoon for a month. The children, well, they were pre-teens—"

"Tweenies," she says.

•

"—couldn't wait for the next part." I try not to sound impatient.

"At the rate you're going," she says, *"I'm surprised it didn't take a whole year. Well? The mother's making tea for the merchant. Sigh."*

Amar showed him the rooms in which the brothers had slept. One housed dogs and cats, horses and cows, even tigers and dragons. A second room was a brittle garden of flowers like jasmine and water lily. In a corner lay a branch covered with cherry blossoms. A third room held tiny people from every walk of life from warrior to peasant to priest.

Upon returning to the main room, Tambunan sank dreamily onto a mat. He accepted a cup from Amar's mother. The first sip restored his frown.

"Hmm, pretty little things," he said, "but hardly precious. Your mother's right. They have no value. Still, why don't you let me take a sample from each room to Edhone? That's where I'm bound. I'll do my best to sell them."

"They're not for sale," Amar said. "They're only for enjoyment."

"What?" his mother snapped. "My lord, he doesn't know what he's saying!"

Tambunan half closed his eyes to set her at ease. Then he beamed at Amar. "Tell me, my friend," Tambunan asked, "how will people in towns enjoy your work unless you sell it? You don't strike me as selfish. I'll make sure only the most appreciative buy your work. Not collectors of trinkets. In return I'll keep a third—no, say a half—of what they fetch. If you don't want to soil your fingers with silver, I can give you notes promising rice. You can give them to your mother if you wish. Don't you want to help her?"

Amar tried to say, "Of course—"

His mother silenced him with a glare. "Silver will be fine," she told Tambunan. "My other sons raise all the rice we need. They break their backs like their father did." She told Amar, "Think of all the prayers your work will buy for him. Would you squander a gift from the gods?"

"Very well," he said.

And so Tambunan resumed his journey to Edhone. He went by palanquin instead of by foot. On his lap lay three of Amar's carvings wrapped in cotton. Tambunan returned a week later with three pieces of silver, which he reverently placed in Amar's palm.

Amar could not hide his disbelief. He gave the silver to his mother and three more carvings to Tambunan. This time he was bound for his home in Makura.

"That definitely sounds Japanese," my wife says. "And Edhone sounds a lot like Edo. Was that the old name for Tokyo?"

"It might have been," I say. "I don't remember."

"The class system sounds Japanese, too. Peasants were higher than merchants in medieval Japan."

"How do you know such things?"

"I do read," she says. "I'm not sure changing a name here or there makes this story feel any less Japanese. Didn't you say once that the difference between an amateur and a professional is that an amateur's work gels too fast? While a professional's stays … fluid. Maybe this story gelled too fast."

"Or maybe it took on a life of its own," I suggest.

"Have it your way," she says. "Well? Then what happened?"

"Well," I say. "If you insist."

Poor, foolish Amar. He knew nothing about rice except how to eat it, and even less about silver.

Upon reaching Edhone with the first three carvings, Tambunan had taken lodgings at its finest inn. He let it be known that for one piece of silver, or the equivalent in notes, he would give a private viewing of the finest work in the kingdom. Between sunrise and sunset, a dozen of the town's wealthiest citizens visited the inn. All of them left with light hearts and glazed eyes. The following day, he sold the carvings—not to those who could pay the highest prices, but to those who would continue buying from him. He earned three pieces of gold, nine pieces of silver, and notes promising thirty bushels of rice. On his next journey through the village, he wore new clothes. His robe, though outwardly plain as the law demanded of merchants, was lined with brocade.

Amar's mother ooh-ed and aah-ed.

Amar guessed the source of Tambunan's wealth but politely ignored it. He remained content knowing people gazed at his works and forgot their everyday cares while composing poetry or listening to the sound of one hand clap. At last his brothers left him alone while he sat carving. Women bowed when they passed on the way to the well. Still, it is the fate of the young that when they reach their goal they fix their eyes on another. So it happened with Amar. His peace of mind lasted one winter and melted with the snow.

2

Daughter of the Sun

ONE DAY IN EARLY SPRING, Amar heard a commotion near the well. "Put down your tools for once," his eldest brother called. He was running past the house. "The emperor's messenger is here."

After all the villagers had gathered, the messenger read an edict in a haughty voice. He barely paused to breathe. "As has been its custom since the time of Emperor Jimmu Tenno, whose grandsire was sent to earth by the Sun Goddess Amaterasu, the imperial family will soon leave its winter home in the City That Floats to spend the summer in Fire Palace on the slope of Fire Mountain. Since the imperial family has chosen to rest in this village on the night before its ascent, you are commanded to have everything in readiness. Furthermore, every unmarried man below the rank of warrior must hide himself on the great day since Princess Meena, Daughter of the Sun, will for the first time accompany her imperial father."

The village had never known such a busy spring. Mothers made new clothes for their families. Builders painted beams and patched walls. Masons recobbled the main road. Only the peasants like Amar's brothers did little, real work. They feared the emperor might raise their taxes if their paddies looked too green, so they spent their evenings making kites for their children and tying streamers to eaves.

·

Everyone except Amar talked about the great day. In the midst of all the chatter, he carved. On Tambunan's next journey through the village, Amar showed him the musical instruments he had crafted to mark the imperial visit.

Tambunan sighed while holding a lute. It was so true to life, it sang when his breath passed over its strings. "Fire Palace has the finest view in our kingdom of the constellations," he said. "Yet for one glimpse of Princess Meena, I would agree to never again look at the stars. Her face is as pale as the moon, but her eyes blaze like suns. I've heard that if any unmarried man of humble origin looked at her, he would fall in love at once. Thus, the emperor's edict. If only we had the spines of warriors! They love, but they never fall in love. Ah, the poetry I could compose in her honour."

"Why don't you ever write poems for me?" my wife asks.

"What? Oh, I'm not a romantic, I guess."

"But you tell love stories," she says. "You can see from a mile away that Amar's going to fall in love with the princess."

"But what kind of story would it be if he didn't fall in love with her?" Inspiration strikes. "Here's a poem for you."

"I'm all ears."

"It's pretty short."

"Stop stalling," she says.

"It's called 'A Tweedy Lass from Peebles—'"

"That's in Scotland, not in Japan. Oh, all right. Sweep me off my feet." But she seems unimpressed while I recite:

Her eyes, they were a squilly blue;

Her cheeks, a dusky, daffy hue;

Her lips, a rose incarnadine.

I plucked her thorns and made her mine.

"Maybe you should stick to stories," my wife says.

•

I moan, "Another budding poet nipped in the—"

"Where were we?" she asks. "Oh, yes. Lowly bachelors fall in love with Meena at first sight. By the way, in case you didn't know it, married men live longer than bachelors."

Amar shrugged. "Warriors are different from us only because they train in different arts," he said. "We are all of the same stock. Why, from a stone I can carve either a warrior or a priest. It merely depends on the flaws."

Amar's mother opened her mouth to scold him, but Tambunan bowed over his cup. "I forgot what a man of the world you are," he said. "After all, you can capture a person's soul in his likeness." When Amar's lips tightened at this barb, Tambunan oiled his voice with a chuckle. "No, you would not fall in love with the princess. As a peasant, you are of higher station than a mere merchant. Indeed, I can think of no one in the kingdom better suited for her than you, my friend."

Amar's mother served Tambunan more tea. "Whatever do you mean?" she asked.

"Why," Tambunan said, "your son and the princess both have magic powers. Your son breathes life into wood and stone. The princess makes the finest cloth in the kingdom. Using her bare hands, she spins a thread called … silk. From raindrops. Then she wraps different colours of thread about her fingers and weaves her cloth in mid-air. Only those of imperial blood may wear this silk."

"Now, that's a nice touch," my wife says.

Tambunan's flattery annoyed Amar but he could not put the princess from his thoughts. Respected by the villagers, he now felt himself as worthy as any warrior. The idea grew in his mind that he truly might be suited to the princess. To speak with her

.

even if she hid behind a bamboo screen, as he had heard ladies at court did, would be more than he could hope for. But by defying the emperor's edict, he could at least see her. "Then I can judge whether her beauty is a myth," he thought. "And whether I have the spine of a warrior."

On the evening the imperial family reached the village, all but one of its lowly, unmarried men remained indoors. Amar laid out his bedroll and stuffed it with rags. He climbed out the window, then made for the low hill behind the inn. With his knees bent and his knuckles grazing the earth, he looked like a monkey scurrying from house to tree to wall. Blossoms nodded everywhere. Breezes tinkled chimes. Yet he saw nothing except the hill and heard nothing except his own heart beat. He scampered up the hill and hid in the shadows of a boulder at the foot of a tree.

Soon, from the far end of the village, there came the brassy clang of cymbals and rhythmic thump of drums. The villagers cheered when the imperial family entered the town. Over the rooftops a hundred colourful kites, no two the same, marked the main road. After what seemed like an age, the procession came into sight: first, the musicians; then, three dozen mounted warriors with bows and quivers slung on their backs; next, the village headman and its priest, who proudly walked in front of three palanquins. Carried by swarthy men, these palanquins bore the emperor and his concubines. Then came the chief warrior. Then, a single palanquin on whose lacquered roof blazed a red and gold lotus. More warriors followed, these on foot, as did courtiers and servants, cooks and maids.

Amar kept his eyes on the lone palanquin. He could see only the fan the princess fluttered in front of her face. And one, small hand. The first three palanquins stopped in front of the inn, at the foot of the hill. The innkeeper and his wife, waiting at the gate on their knees, bowed low. The emperor stepped onto raked pebbles. He gestured for the princess's palanquin to be brought to the gate. Amar held his breath. A wisp of cloud passed over the setting sun. He shivered. When the chief warrior offered his arm, the princess grasped it and closed her fan. Then, while the cloud uncovered the sun, she faced the hill. "That old devil!" Amar exclaimed. "Tambunan was right." The princess's face looked so exquisite, a master carver might have chiselled it from ivory. But Tambunan had been wrong about her eyes. They did not blaze like suns. They were two dark pools of sorrow.

The emperor also offered her his arm. Slowly, with the chief warrior on her left and her father on her right, she stepped to earth. Tears filled Amar's eyes until she seemed to move through mists rising from the lake.

Meena had glossy, black hair longer than she was tall. It had been coiled on her head, held in place with golden pins and combs, then allowed to cascade over her shoulders. She wore a dozen silk robes. Those beneath had sleeves longer than those on top, and each robe was a different shade: orange, apricot, tangerine, peach. Brushing the ground as they did, the sleeves looked like wings. A black sash at her tiny waist matched her hair. Black slippers covered her feet.

"If she's not Japanese," my wife says, "what is she?"

"A princess. I didn't say those robes were kimonos, did I?"

"Well," she says, "they're certainly not saris."

"Funny you should mention that. When I first showed this story to my mentor, he asked me why it wasn't set in India. I said, 'Because I don't know anything about India.' And he said, 'What about the mother, then?

Why couldn't she be an Indian mother?' And I said, 'Oh, no. An Indian mother would have a much sharper tongue—'"

"You said what!" my wife asks. *"Even you wouldn't stoop to such stereotypes."*

"It's not a matter of stereotypes," I insist. "It's a matter of conventions, and this is a conventional story."

"You can say that again."

"But here's the best part. My mentor laughed and said, 'See, you do know something about India.'"

"Speaking within conventions, of course," my wife says.

"Speaking within the world of this particular story."

"Whatever. So what about this geisha doll princess?"

Amar wanted to run to her. The archers might shoot him long before he reached the inn, but he would die a happy man if he could hold her for even a moment; if he could feel her arms wrap him in their silken warmth and watch the sadness in her eyes replaced with delight. And yet, he could not move. When the moon sparkled on the lake, he realized he had been hiding for hours. The princess had long ago entered the inn. The warriors had pitched their camps outside the gate. The courtiers had bedded down in the village's finer houses. He returned home with little care for his safety. He lay down and slept like a man who had climbed a mountain.

Next morning, his mother took a long time to serve their meal. She said the younger concubine's maid had reminded her of herself on her wedding day. "That's nothing compared to how Princess Meena will look at her wedding." His mother sighed. "The Lords of Makura and Edhone are such lucky men to be allowed to vie for her hand."

Amar stopped shovelling boiled greens into his mouth.

.

"What did you say?"

"Daydreaming again?" his mother asked. "The younger concubine's maid told the innkeeper's wife, who told the rest of us. Meena reaches the age of womanhood this summer. The emperor chose his chief warrior for her. But strong-willed girl she's become since her mother died, Meena demanded the right to marry into one of the kingdom's finest houses. The Lords of Makura and Edhone will have to prove themselves at arms, at composing poetry, at—"

Amar dropped his bowl. It left a trail of greens while rolling on the mat. He felt as though he had swallowed his heart and might spew it up in pieces.

"What's the matter?" his mother cried.

He dashed from the house. He ran through the village to the inn. He ran past the inn up to the boulder and tree. From here he stared at Fire Mountain. Morning mists shrouded the palace. Clutching his stomach, he sank to his knees. He pressed his burning brow against cool moss. "The villagers were right," he groaned. "I am useless. How can I hope to win a princess in tests of arms when I'm not even allowed to carry a sword? All my precious creations won't buy a word with her." He rolled onto his back and watched sun beams pierce the mist near the palace.

Running his fingers over the rough bark and mossy stone, he recalled his gift from the gods. "What good will it do me now?" he wondered. "Artists at court make beautiful things everyday." His spine tingled while he sensed the life in the wood and stone. Through the bark, he could see grain. Through the moss, veins of crystal. "True, my carvings are different," he mused. "One masterpiece: that's all I need. I may not be able to vie for my beloved, but I can still gain an audience at court." His despair

·

vanished, and the rising sun burned the mist off the mountain. "Yes," he cried, "I'll make a gift for the emperor. Surely then he will see how much I love his daughter and give her to me? Surely then I will prove that even a peasant can win a princess for his bride!"

"Poor, foolish Amar is right," my wife says. "This is a set up if I've ever heard one."

Now I do sound impatient when I say, "You haven't heard anything yet."

Her hair, which is still a strawberry blonde, glints when she tosses her head. She intones, "Beware the storyteller who sings praises of his own story."

"Thanks a lot," I say. "You've gone and ended this chapter on an unstressed syllable."

•

3

Fire Palace

IN THE WEEKS FOLLOWING the imperial visit, Amar became the happiest and most miserable of men. His love for the princess grew into a fierce wind churning a wave of joy in his heart. He imagined himself turning into a light, colourful creature that could float from flower and tree to mountain and cloud. Then he remembered he was an earthbound man. The wave of joy crashed. At such times he climbed to the tree, stared at Fire Palace, and tried to summon the wind. As magical as his work was, nothing he carved seemed fit to present at court—not the lotus with sunbeam petals, not the warrior whose passion threatened to burst from his flesh. At last he decided to carve something never before seen by ordinary eyes. But what? He searched for the answer day and night until his eyes burned and his hands shook. He cursed the gods for decreeing that, although he and Princess Meena might be alike, she should dwell in the clouds while he should plod among men.

One warm, summer day he sat brooding on the hill. The wind rippled across paddies and turned them into squares of green brocade: one moment, light; another, dark. He looked everywhere for inspiration. He searched in the clouds, in the waves of Moon Lake, in the creatures about him. A dragonfly hovered near the rock. Its wings twinkled with different colours,

·

but its all-seeing eyes disturbed him. "Why," he wondered, "are there so few beautiful insects? Why do so many have slimy bodies, or pincers or stings? And why are they all so useful? Is there no insect, is there no creature on earth meant to be simply beautiful?" He conjured up his vision of Princess Meena. For the hundredth time, she stepped from her palanquin with her arms outstretched and her sleeves, like wings, fluttering in the breeze—

Amar whooped. The dragonfly fled. "All this time I've been trying to carve what she means to me," he cried. "The nearest I've come is her symbol, the sun-like lotus. Why not carve Meena herself?" He laughed and shouted at the palace, "Your Imperial Highness, in return for your daughter's hand you'll receive from me her very likeness!" The fierce wind swelled the wave of joy in his heart. He ran home to begin his work.

"I like dragonflies," my wife says. "They're not repulsive."

"No, they're beautiful," I agree. "The way their wings twinkle in the sun—"

"But if you juxtapose the dragonfly with slimy bodied insects—you're probably thinking of worms, and worms aren't insects—you'll give children the wrong impression."

"I needed a way for him to wonder whether there's any creature on earth meant to be simply beautiful."

"Like Meena," my wife says.

"Like you," I insist.

"Don't push your luck," she says. She's changing from a strawberry blonde into a redhead.

"Anyway," I tell her, "this isn't a children's story."

"Then why did you tell it to those tweenies?" She has such a good memory—my wife. "And why did your editor put it in that anthology of songs and poems and stories for children. The one he co-edited with—"

•

"Editor, co-editor—whose story is this, anyway?"

"Touché," my wife concedes. *"But this is all beside the point. If Amar thinks dragonflies aren't beautiful—"*

"I never said that!"

"—I can't say I think much of his aesthetic sensibilities. Oh, stop scowling and get on with it. I have to get to work. So do you, upstairs."

Yet by the end of the day, Amar despaired. No wood was hard enough, no stone flawless enough to capture Meena's fragile beauty. Only one thing could, and he would have to ask for help.

During Tambunan's next visit, Amar revealed what he sought.

"Jade?" Tambunan asked.

"Not just jade. Flawless, pink jade."

Amar's mother stared at him. "You've been acting oddly," she said, "but this is the silliest thing I've heard."

"And what will you give me to sell for this rare stone?" Tambunan asked.

Amar dropped his eyes to the leaves floating in his tea. "Nothing I've carved in these past few weeks is good enough to show people," he claimed. "I smashed it all."

"There is still the peacock," his mother said.

"That was a gift to my father," he reminded her. "You cannot part with it. It's all you have left to remember him by."

"It seems I must part with it," she said, "for I see this jade means much to you. Besides, the peacock isn't all I have left of your father. I still have you and your brothers."

Tambunan spread his hands. "Again you amaze me," he said. "How could anyone carve a peacock? Its tail feathers would break."

Amar's mother rose and entered her sleeping room. After returning with the carving, she placed it in front of Tambunan.

.

Amar had carved the peacock from a glassy, black stone. The tail feathers were so delicate, they shivered in the slightest breeze. They whispered like spirits in the dark.

Tambunan's fingers twitched. He bit a knuckle to keep from laughing. He knew this one treasure would earn him as much as all the rest had earned. He wiped his sweaty palms on his thighs. "I don't know why you want this jade," he said, "but you'll get it. The finest in the kingdom."

For once, Tambunan was as good as his word.

Amar set to work. He had carved the gift so many times in his dreams, he could have done it blindfolded. Yet he worked carefully, for he knew the quiver of a finger might shatter the stone. He worked not on the veranda but in his room, closed even to his mother's worried eyes. Before starting work each day, he gazed at the jade until the figure he sought glowed from within. Then he chipped away stone to bring the warm heart to the surface. On the day a soft pink light flooded his room, he knew he had freed the carving from the stone.

"That's a nice touch, too," my wife says.

On midsummer's day, the Lords of Makura and Edhone met at the village inn. Each rode at the head of a dozen, mounted warriors. A crowd gathered at a respectful distance to watch, but Amar approached the inn on his knees. He wore his best, purple robes. In a trembling voice, he offered to lead the lords up the mountain to the palace.

"Yes, we need a guide," said the young Lord of Makura. He adjusted his eagle-winged helmet.

"What payment do you wish?" asked the Lord of Edhone. He beat the dust from his travelling cloak with a horsetail whisk.

"To walk behind you through my village and before you up

·

the mountain will be my reward," Amar said. "I am unworthy of any payment."

The lords agreed.

Amar waited until the last horse passed him before he followed. He held a rosewood box close to his chest so the horse's tail could not flick the box from his grasp. He had inlaid the wood with jade chips and shaped the box around his gift like a velvet hand. Tightlipped, his eyes feverish, he ignored his brothers' disapproving stares while he passed their fields. "When I return with the princess," he thought, "they will all have to kneel. I won't let them. Enough of this bowing and scraping! Then again, perhaps I will make them kneel. Didn't they laugh at me all those years?" With his heart and mind in turmoil, he ran ahead to lead the lords from the humid shores of Moon Lake up the cool slope of Fire Mountain. He had never taken this path; yet he moved with such sureness, the lords followed him blindly.

By late afternoon, the procession reached Fire Palace. Its outer walls looked so red, they glowed at sunrise and sunset. Its eaves, upswept like wings, made one think it could take to the air. While the lords and their warriors entered the courtyard, drums beat in welcome.

Amar walked past the guards at the gate. Remaining close to the outer walls, he hid himself among the servants.

The lords and warriors dismounted, then gave their horses to grooms. The warriors took their places in front of a large, open veranda attached to the main hall. The lords stepped onto the veranda itself. Everyone waited: the lords in front, the warriors behind, the courtiers next, the servants last. At a signal from the emperor's chief warrior, they knelt and sat back on their heels. A gilt door opened. The imperial family appeared. Like one man, the assembly touched its forehead to the ground. Still like one man, the assembly straightened its back.

Amar swallowed while staring at the servant in front of him. He was sure everyone could hear his heart pound like a signal drum. "What am I doing here?" he wondered. Then he dared to raise his eyes.

The emperor was dressed in silk robes the colour of a gathering storm. He bore the sacred symbols of power: the mirror and the sword. A thin, gold band held a radiant sun on his brow. Princess Meena stood next to him. She looked even lovelier than she had the first time Amar had seen her. Now her dozen robes were shades of pink, her sash and slippers the colour of burnt almond. Once again, though, he saw sadness in her eyes.

He rose. He stumbled past the servants and courtiers, even past the warriors, before two guards crossed bronze-tipped spears in front of him.

The lords turned with their hands on their hilts.

The emperor squinted at Amar's sandals. They were made of rice straw. "Who is this peasant?" he calmly asked. "What does he want?"

"Only to present a gift to Your Imperial Highness," Amar said. "Forgive me for disrupting your ceremony, but I could not wait." He placed the box on the veranda and knelt on the ground. Clutching the crossed spears like the bars of a prison, he pressed his brow against them. "I am Amar," he said. "From the village on the shore of Moon Lake, which washes your imperial feet."

A movement of the emperor's mirror parted the spears.

The Lords of Makura and Edhone moved aside.

"Well," the emperor said, "open it."

Amar undid the brass clasp. He opened the box and gingerly

lifted out his gift. He placed it at the emperor's feet, bowed, and knelt once more.

Everyone gasped. Those in the back forgot themselves and half rose for a better view. Not only had they never seen such a lovely carving, but they had also never seen such a strange creature. Six, thin legs held its slender body off the ground. Huge wings sprouted from each side of the body. Not long, curved, birdlike wings but flat, wide ones. They were veined like leaves.

The emperor knelt and passed his hand under a wing. Amar had made it so thin, the emperor could read the lines of his palm through the jade. Rising slowly, as if in a dream, he said, "Truly ..."

"Unique?" the Lord of Makura suggested.

"Priceless," the Lord of Edhone said.

"What is it?" the emperor asked.

They politely shrugged.

Amar heard courtiers and servants ask the same question. Only the warriors were silent. They remained unmoved, like statues. When a faint smile curved the princess's lips, Amar thought, "She knows."

"Well," the emperor said, "no descendant of the Sun Goddess can receive such a gift without giving a unique and priceless one in return." He nodded his thanks to both of the lords. "What is your fondest wish?" he asked Amar. "To serve me and carve the imperial sun on all your works? To be headman of your village?"

A great calm settled on Amar's mind. Now that what he had dreamt of possessing stood within his grasp, he pretended to think about his answer. He stood. He raised his arm toward Princess Meena and said, "I want the hand of your daughter in marriage."

A hush fell on the gathering.

•

Then the entire court, including the warriors, burst into laughter. The laughter burned Amar's ears but he kept his head high, his back straight.

The emperor raised the mirror to his lips, and the laughter died. Courtiers coughed behind fans. "You must be mad," he said, "to think you could vie with these lords. Even if my daughter admired you for your skill, do you not realize a princess must hold her duty above her feelings?"

"Imperial Highness," Amar cried, "noble as they are, these lords see your daughter as nothing more than a step to your throne. All they understand is the way of the sword. Knowing how to kill a man is not enough, even if one then writes a poem with his blood."

The young lords growled at these words.

Amar told Meena, "I can offer you happiness. I can free you from all these fans and robes, this measured speech. You will give me inspiration to carve even more wondrous things. We are alike, you and I, for only we know what this strange creature is. You've seen it countless times in mirrors. I saw it for the first time when you stayed at our inn."

She nodded ever so slightly, and his heart leapt.

"Hold it right there!" my wife says.

I groan, "But we're getting to the best part!"

"Fine, this is supposed to be a conventional story, but does it have to be so ... patriarchal? 'You will give me inspiration to carve even more wondrous things.' Oh, please!"

"Funny you should mention that," I say. "That's exactly why my latest editor suggested I drop this story from my new collection. She said the others deal with men and women in a more enlightened way. With ... what do you call it?"

"Gender relations," my wife suggests.

"I don't have a head for fancy terms and theories," I say. "There's postmodern, postcolonial, posthypnotic—"

"Look," she says. "I'll accept that these characters exist within a rigid, hierarchical framework, but how can Amar free Meena if she goes from being a chattel to being a muse?"

"Maybe I'm trying to be ironic," I say.

"Maybe you're trying to cop out." She adds, "What this story needs is a feminist twist. Like Angela Carter's stories about Little Red Riding Hood and the Big Bad Wolf."

"That wolf's from someone else's story," I say. "The one with the three Little Pigs. According to Bruno Bettelheim—"

"I thought you didn't have a head for theories?"

"I don't," I insist. "But we're still getting to the best part."

"Take it easy," she says. "Okay, Amar reveals that he saw Meena, after all. She nods. His heart leaps."

The chief warrior strode forward. "You defied the emperor's edict?" he demanded. "For that, the penalty is death!" Before Amar could draw back, the warrior whipped his sword from its scabbard and drew a wide circle before him. The blade sliced through Amar. The burning pain that filled his heart turned to numbing despair. His knees buckled. He raised his arms to appeal to the princess. Even as life drained from his body, his arms arced downward. His leaden hands smashed the carving, and Amar fell dead.

"What!" my wife shrieks. "How could you!"

4

Meena's Gift

"I DIDN'T DO IT," I SAY. "The story did. The story wrote itself."

"Here we go again with that metaphysical stuff," my wife scoffs. "No wonder you'll never make deputy minister. You scare them half to death with your voices dictating cabinet documents."

"Remember what you said?" I tell her. "Anyone could see from a mile off that Amar would fall in love with Meena. Well, then, they should've known he couldn't get away with defying the emperor's edict."

"But still," my wife says. "Amar's dead. The magical carving is smashed. What's left to tell? You don't kill off your main character three-quarters of the way in."

"Angela Carter might. You said it needed a feminist twist."

"This is not an Angela Carter story," my wife says. "It's too nice. Or it was. Plus there's no eroticism." Her hair is glinting again. Copper is flashing among the reds.

"Oh," I say. "Well, if it's eroticism you want, what about this?"

Meena felt a ripple beneath her feet. The earth stood still, and time itself stopped. Yet when they both began moving once more, Amar did not rise. He lay slumped at her father's feet with one hand resting on the shattered jade.

The courtiers muttered their appreciation of the chief warrior's skill. When he wiped his blade on Amar's robes, blood stained the purple cloth. "Great One," he said, bowing, "Grandson of the Sun, I regret having acted so rashly, but I could not bear the affront to your law. I would gladly pay with my life for drawing my sword without permission; yet what can I offer in return for destroying this gift with my clumsiness?"

The emperor gazed at Amar's body for a long time before replying. "I can excuse your rashness," he said, "for a warrior must have fire in his veins. Fire created us. Fire rules us. However, for destroying one of my possessions, I decree you must be untouchable until sunrise tomorrow. Carry this peasant to his village on your own back, and bury him yourself."

The chief warrior paled, for he would be shamed among his men, but he dropped his sword. When he moved toward the body, Meena tossed her fan on the ground. Not daring to let his shadow fall across her fan, he backed away.

She stepped down from the veranda and lifted Amar to his feet. When she removed her hands, his body stood by itself.

"What are you doing?" the emperor asked.

She said nothing. Tears welled in her eyes. After gathering shards of jade, she rubbed her hands to create a fine, pink powder, which she pressed into Amar's wound. The sword cut faded.

Again the emperor opened his mouth but, this time, he did not speak.

Though she knew it was shameful to do so, Meena wept. She welcomed the tears, for they softened the harsh world by bathing it in mist. She thought her heart would finally break. Amar had been the first man to dream of freeing her from her silk and gold prison; yet he had been killed as a criminal. Staring at musicians near the gate, she willed them to play. Eyebrows rose when she began to dance. While her tears fell, she spun them into the glistening silk for which she was famed. She wove it around Amar. Circle after circle, she danced her slow dance. She wove her magical cloth. When the thread snagged on sunbeams, flecks of gold settled on the shroud. She wove the last thread into place.

A guard climbed down from his tower and dropped to his knees. "Great One," he said, "all the trees on the shore of Moon Lake have blossomed!"

The emperor scoffed. "In the middle of the summer? The time of flies and dust in the low lands? All the blossoms wilted soon after we arrived."

The guard pressed his forehead to the ground. "Forgive me," he said. "These feeble eyes must have played tricks on me." He raised his head. "But I saw blossoms everywhere: apple white, cherry pink, peach, and plum. It's a miracle!"

The emperor looked at Meena. "No," he said, "it is only magic."

"I like that," my wife says. "'It's only magic.'"

The shroud quivered. It swelled. It shrank. The movements grew so violent, the shroud toppled to the ground. It lay still. Then it grew faint at one end as though being eaten away from within. When Amar's head emerged, everyone except Meena drew back. Fear gripped their hearts.

Amar no longer resembled a man. His eyes had moved to the sides of his head. His ears had grown thin and knobbed. His nose had grown long and lay coiled under his chin. His mouth had vanished. Using spindly, black arms, he pulled his body from the shroud. He had grown long and thin and now had six legs. Most amazing of all, he had sprouted two pairs of broad, veined wings. At first they lay curled about his body. Then, while the sun warmed them, they straightened. They rustled like fans. Dark purple above, flecked with orange and white, the wings were many-coloured below: purple, violet, red-orange, white. They hardened in the sun.

At last, Meena spoke. "Behold the butterfly. He has no duty but to delight the eye."

The courtiers and servants muttered among themselves:

"What is it called?"

"A but-ter-fly."

"What does it do?"

"Nothing, she said. It's so beautiful, why should it do anything?"

My wife smiles to humour me. She looks as if she's about to mention chores again but she says, "Don't you dare stop."

Meena turned to her suitors. "And what duty would I have except to delight your eyes?" she asked. "I could change one of you from lord into consort, but what would you do for me? You would save your true love for concubines, just as my father did. Great One," she told him, "I cannot wed either of them. The only man I could ever have married was this gentle peasant, who saw me for what I am: a delicate, useless creature. True, I have one power beyond your reach, but I have lessened it with my own hand. Now that silk has been spun from tears, it can never be as precious as before. Anyone can learn the art. The old ways are dying."

The emperor gazed steadfastly over her head.

"Father," she cried, "are you listening? I would sooner marry a merchant and be free than let you award me to one of these peacocks!"

Her words startled him, and he dropped the sacred mirror. It shattered. His face contorted with pain while he stared at the shards of silvered glass. "Falling and breaking," he whispered. "Everything is falling and … No!" He planted his feet wide apart.

•

They seemed to take root. "If you do not marry one of these lords and give me an heir, my house itself will fall! This cannot be. If only by bloodying the sacred sword, if only by breaking tradition can I preserve the old ways, so be it. How wonderful will you think your lover if he has no wings?" The emperor drew his sword.

In the time it took him to raise the sword above his head, to grasp its hilt with both hands, Meena moved to protect Amar. "Fly!" she said. "Spend your new life bringing colour into ours: lives all the more dreary for the trappings we wear, for the hours wasted on ceremony. I am imprisoned but you, my love, are free."

With a single flap of his wings, Amar took to the air. His flight was not as graceful as a bird's. He zigged and zagged, rose and fell. Yet the sunlight on his wings dazzled all eyes.

The emperor's hands grew numb. When he dropped the sacred sword, his face turned red with shame, then grey like his robes. "Archers," he called, "shoot down that beast!"

Meena screamed, "No!"

The archers bent their bows and shot. When a single arrow grazed Amar's wing, he let out a shrill cry. Echoing from the clouds to the lake, it woke the spirits of Fire Mountain.

Smoke rose from the crater: first in wisps, then in streams, then in thick, grey columns that hid the sun. Villagers ran from their houses and huddled about the well. Hot wind swirled down the slope and stripped leaves from trees yet left the blossoms untouched. Like a giant waking from centuries of sleep, the mountain shuddered. The palace walls cracked. A guard tower fell. When the spirits finally vented their rage, the summit exploded. Not suddenly like a thundercloud, but ever so slowly. The mountain gathered power from the depths of the earth. When it could no longer contain such force, it spewed a ball

·

of fiery rock. The rock scorched the clouds. Then it fell on the palace. While the main hall collapsed, its eaves fluttered like the wings of a huge, dying moth.

Only then did anyone move. With no thought for decorum, emperor and warrior, courtier and servant—all dashed for safety. They could not escape, for sheets of burning ash rained upon them. Refusing to betray their fear, the Lords of Makura and Edhone smothered. They froze into ashen statues.

Meena remained untouched. With the palace burning behind her and the outer walls crumbling about her, she, too, refused to flee. She searched through the gloom for one last glimpse of Amar. When he flitted downward, through the fiery rain, a great wave grew in her heart. She raised her arms, and he crushed her to his body. Even as they rose into clear, blue sky, the spirits buried the palace under cinders and ash.

Yet Meena and Amar did not fly alone. While children squealed with delight, the blossoms came to life as butterflies. Orange, purple, white and pink, they fluttered like rice-paper fans; like shimmering, gossamer rainbows. The wind scattered them up the slopes of Fire Mountain, over Moon Lake, and throughout the Kingdom of the Sun. The end.

My wife laughs with delight. The love of my life—she laughs with delight. "I should've known the butterfly would show up when you mentioned silk early on," she says. "Still, I'm glad you didn't call this story 'How the Butterfly Got Its Wings.'"

"So am I," I tell her, "even if that's one of the things the story decided it would be about. I couldn't—"

"Stories deciding! Don't start that again. Tell me something, though: where do you get your ideas?"

She asks me where I get my ideas, and there she sits changing from a redhead back into a brunette. I'm sure she's not humouring me—she has better things to do—so I tell her: "I was visiting a friend at a writers/artists' colony once. We went for a walk. I saw two yellow butterflies and said, 'Has anyone written a story about butterflies?' He said, 'Vladimir Nabokov has, but don't let that stop you.'"

"There you go dropping names again," my wife says. "First Carter, now Nabokov. Then there's the editor and the friend—"

"But all these people were important to me. They still are. Not Nabokov. Can't get into him, somehow. But did I mention that writer-in-residence at the public library? I kept taking him stories and none of them came up to scratch. But the day he read this one, he left messages all over town just to tell me I'd broken through. Finally."

This time she intones, "Beware the storyteller who sings praises of his own perseverance."

"I'm not a storyteller," I say. "I'm a story writer. There's a difference."
"Such as?"
"Such as ... I like you best as a brunette."

"Don't get cute," she says. "Oh, look at the time! If you're not going to start on the toilet today, you might as well mow the lawn. Don't look so put out. Even a storyteller ... sorry, a story writer has to live in the real world." After she heads outside, I follow her as far as the door and say:

"Guess I'll feed the cat first."

When she reaches the car, she stops and calls, "We don't have a cat. You're allergic to cats." Then, standing there hefting the car keys, she says, "Oh, no! You haven't gone and made up a cat!"

•

RAINBOW KNIGHTS

1

Strange Fortune

ONCE UPON A TIME there lived a fisherman named William on the edge of the Northern Sea. People called him Bowman because, in his youth, he had been the best archer on the coast. He had helped defend it many a time from invasion by seafaring Northmen.

To mark five years of peace, the Duke of Castle Fen granted William a boon.

"What's a boon?" Our daughter, Gillian, asks this without turning from her plush elephant. His name is Mr. Allenby, don't ask me why.

"It's like a favour," I say. "Actually, it's a blessing, and it comes from an Old Norse word that means petition."

"Oh."

"Sire," William said, "a fisherman should live within sight of the sea. Let me build a cottage outside the town walls, where I can hear the waves and feel the wind."

The duke thought for a moment, then nodded. "Our king gave me this land to rule. Now I give you the shore. But it's yours only as long as your house serves mine." He gave William a glove as a token of their bond.

The following spring, William built a one-room cottage near the water's edge. That summer, he married his childhood sweetheart, Alison Fair.

Gillian giggles. "Mommy's name is Alice! Is she in this story?"

"Where would we be without Mommy?"

They worked from dawn till dusk and rarely went hungry. William fished six days a week. When high waves threatened to upset his boat, he hunted wildfowl in the marsh. Alison cooked their meals, made and mended their clothes, and tended their garden and hencoop. After a year she gave birth to a boy. He had hair as golden as flax and eyes blue-green like the sea. William named him Nigel. After Nigel learned to walk, he followed William everywhere. The boy even went fishing, though Alison said Nigel was still too young. She feared he might tumble overboard.

"A cottage is no place for a boy," William said. "He must learn to love the sea."

Nigel had the curiosity of a kitten and asked question after question: "Why is the sky blue? Where does the sun go at night?" Alison replied as best she could. William thought it strange that the son of a fisherman did not ask more useful questions like, "Where is the best place to fish?"

"Daddy," Gillian cries, "I'm not a boy! You said I was the hero of this story!"

"You are, my sweet. But the hero doesn't always show up right away. I told you this was a long story."

"What about Mr. Allenby?"

"I'm sure he'll turn up sooner or later."

On Nigel's fourth birthday, Alison took him to the town. While William sold his catch, she bought Nigel a sweetroll. Just then, the duke rode through the marketplace. Armed horsemen followed him. Everyone cheered the duke but Nigel had eyes only for the horsemen. He admired the mail shining under their colourful tunics—

"Our mailman doesn't ride a horse!"

Someone says from behind me, "Not that kind of mail."

Twisting on the edge of the bed, I find our son, Neil, leaning in Gillian's doorway. With his arms crossed. He pretends he's too old for bedtime stories. "What kind of mail, then?" I ask him.

"Chain mail," he tells Gillian. "Like armour, only..."

"More flexible?" I suggest.

"It bends," he tells her.

I nod at the carpet and ask, "Would you like to join us?"

"Just passing by," he says.

Untwisting, I continue for Gillian's sake, but I make sure my voice carries.

Nigel admired the sunlight flashing off the scabbards. He forgot his sweetroll, and it dropped in the dust. "Who are these men?" he asked.

"They're knights," William replied.

"I'll be one when I grow up!" Nigel said.

"You can't, dear," Alison told him. "Your hair may be golden like a nobleman's, but you'll become a fisherman like your father."

Nigel cried, "I don't want to be a fisherman!"

"No more than I," William muttered. Then he said, "We're commoners with coarse hands. Our hair is dark like the soil. Only the sons of noblemen can become knights."

Alison hugged Nigel and dried his tears. She told William, "He's too young to understand."

Gillian tells Mr. Allenby, "Poor little Nigel."

Neil snorts.

William watched the knights enter the castle. While counting pennies, he told Alison, "Noblemen were commoners once. They won their titles long ago through courage in battle. Now they gain them by luck; by being born in castles instead of cottages. I don't want Nigel to work hard like we do, but the wars have ended. There are no titles to win." He sighed. "Ah, well. I suppose it's better to live in peace than die in battle."

The following day, he and Nigel went to sea. William brooded about his son's lot.

"His what?" Gillian asks.

"His lot in life," Neil says.

"Oh."

Just before sunset, William heard a whisper, drawn out like this: "Will-i-am."

Surprised, he looked about. "Who calls?" he asked.

"The wind. I carry a message from the god of the sea. What would you give to see your son become a knight?"

"Anything! My boat, my strongest bow. The stars and the moon."

"The sun, Will-i-am?"

"Yes, even the sun!"

When the boat began to toss, William grew pale. Fishermen in these parts knew that when waves crested high, it was time to make for land for the god of the sea worked magic that mortals could watch only from shore.

"Mortals are human beings," Neil tells Gillian.

Without turning, I say, "Thank you."

"You sure this is a children's story?" he asks.

"Funny, an editor asked me the same thing," I admit. "Right after she said, 'The average North American child wouldn't understand what a boon is.'"

"And what did you say?"

"That's why we have dictionaries.'"

"Like Neil," Gillian tells Mr. Allenby. "Daddy says Neil's turning into a walking, talking—"

"That's encyclopedia," Neil tells Gillian. "And I am not." Then he tells me, "So. After all this time, you're still smarting over that word boon?"

"Certainly not!" I insist.

He nods to humour me. It's a habit he's picked up from his mother.

Now Gillian announces, "The boat's beginning to toss!"

"This is true," I say.

William told Nigel, "Let's gather the nets." Yet no matter which way William pushed the steerboard, the boat would not turn."

"The tiller," Neil announces.

"They used steerboards in those days," I insist.

Gillian snorts.

The wind blew from every quarter. The sail flapped. The boat creaked. Suddenly, eight sea creatures leapt from the waves. The creatures were blue-grey and smooth-skinned. Squealing together, they seemed to laugh at William.

Nigel found them enchanting. They swam around the boat and dove out of sight. Then, all at once, they shot into the air. He tried to touch one of them, the smallest of the eight. "Look," he said, "they dance on their tails!"

William ordered, "Don't lean so far over the gunwale."

Nigel did not hear the warning. He heard only the creatures' song. They sang of the deep, where seahorses gallop through coral halls. The smallest creature carried a pearl in its mouth. When Nigel reached for this pearl, the wind grew stronger. It became a gale. The boat lurched, the mast snapped, and the sail fell on William. He called to Nigel for help but heard no sound.

•

When William finally threw off the sail, he saw why. His son was gone.

"Oh, no," Gillian cries. She prods Mr. Allenby to make sure he's still awake. "Nigel's been kidnapped!"

"The Dolphin Liberation Front," Neil says.

"Thank you for that," I declare.

"Anytime, Dad."

Shouting Nigel's name, William searched the water around his boat. He pounded the gunwale with his fists. "I've been tricked!" he cried. "I meant I would give the sun in the sky, not my own son!"

"That's a nice twist," Neil says. "But I don't think Gilly gets it."

"I do, too," she says. "There's the s-u-n and the s-o-n."

"And which one is Neil?" I ask her.

"He's the P-I-T-B."

"The what?" I ask.

"That's what Lorna calls him." Lorna is their babysitter. She lives nearby. Neil pretends he's too old for babysitters—which he may be—but he lets her help him with his homework.

"Lorna's just kidding," he tells Gillian.

"But what does it mean?" I ask.

He replies, "You're too old to understand."

Gillian giggles.

Facing her once more, I ask, "Where were we?"

"William's upset," she says.

"I would be, too," I tell her.

Tears streamed down his face. He raised a fist at the wind; yet he dared not invite further sorrow by cursing the god of the sea. "Mortals must accept their fates," he thought. He picked up a paddle and made for shore. Then he heard a squeal and turned.

•

The sea creatures swam toward the setting sun. On the back of the smallest lay Nigel, clutching its fin. The creatures vanished beneath the waves.

Slowly, sadly, William returned home. When he told Alison about the sea creatures' taking Nigel, she cried bitterly. "I wanted the boy to become a knight so badly," William said, "that I lost him. We might never see him again."

"Will ironies never cease?" Neil asks.

I twist to look at him, and he smiles knowingly. Another habit he's picked up from his mother. When he tells us, "I can't wait till I'm done with school," we know what he really means. He means he can't wait till he can leave home, and here he is only twelve. Then again, I couldn't wait either.

"What's going on?" Gillian asks.

"Sorry, my sweet," I say. "I was thinking of another story."

William remembered his nets. "Fool that I am," he told Alison, "I'll lose them to the tide."

He awoke early the next morning. With Alison's help, he mended the boat's mast. He put to sea alone. The nets hung where he had lowered them the day before. They teemed with fish. He never again returned home with empty nets. He and Alison tried to be thankful for the strange fortune that soon made them rich; yet all their gold could not banish their sorrow or buy them news of their son.

Gillian tells Mr. Allenby, "Their s-o-n."

·

2

Gifts from the Sea

FOUR YEARS PASSED. ALL THIS TIME, Alison prayed for another child even as she still grieved over having lost Nigel.

More people left the town to settle near William's cottage. Although the shore belonged to him, he allowed everyone to fish and hunt without paying him taxes. He said, "The fish belong to the god of the sea and the birds to the god of the air. Pay your dues to the duke but none to me."

Proud of his good name, William enlarged the cottage. He replaced its roof of loose straw with one of dry turf. He put aside his shirt of skins and wore one made of cloth. Alison made her dresses from linen now instead of wool. Yet neither of them forgot their humble beginnings as an archer and his wife. They worked six days a week and spent the seventh in the town.

One day, the duke spied them from his castle window. He saw that everyone nodded while passing William and Alison, and so the duke grew jealous. He shouted to his sister, "It's not right!"

"What's the duke's name?" Gillian asks.

"Oh, um, Gerald."

"And his sister?"

"Megan."

Surprised, Gillian sits up. "Uncle Jerry and Aunt Regan! They're in this story, too?"

·

"They are now."

"Quite the family affair," Neil says. "So where are Gillian and I?"

"I said already. Gillian hasn't come into it yet. You've come and gone. Just 'passing by,' remember?"

"You were the horse," Gillian says. "Horsey! Horse—"

I tell her, "Lie down, my sweet. You'll get Mr. Allenby all excited." She does as I ask, and I pull the covers up to her chin. Since Mr. Allenby doesn't like being covered up, I make sure he stays comfortably outside the blanket. He has a thick skin.

"Great," Neil says. "I'm off splashing around with the Dolphin Liberation Front."

"As I was saying?"

Gerald asked Megan, "See how they smile at this commoner? What if their respect for him outweighs their loyalty to me? If a war breaks out, can I trust this Bowman to rally his villagers?"

Megan tried to calm Gerald. "The more respect he earns," she said, "the more important you'll become. You gave him his land. He owes you his wealth and his good name. If you envy him, he'll trouble your dreams."

Fine words, yes, but for all her wisdom, Megan was wrong. William owed his wealth to the god of the sea—who, even now, was training Nigel for knighthood.

"Oh, well," Neil declares. "Why didn't you say so?"

Judging the time ripe to set foot on land, the god of the sea took a mortal's form. One morning, after a stormy night, William found an old man asleep on the beach. William carried him back to the cottage and laid him on a feather mattress in front of the fire.

Alison tried combing the seaweed from the old man's white beard. It was hopelessly tangled. "Is he a sailor?" she asked.

·

"He isn't dressed like one," William said. "I'd say this is a pilgrim's robe."

The old man slept for seven days and nights. On the evening of the eighth day, he awoke. "Where am I?" he asked.

"Near Castle Fen," William replied. "I'm William Bowman. This is my wife, Alison Fair."

"The tide brought you to us a week ago," she said.

"And I slept all that time?" The old man stroked his beard. "How strange!" After dressing in his long, green robe, he joined William and Alison at their table. Having been so long without food, he ate his fill of meat; yet he refused to eat any fish. At last he said, "My name is Alaric."

"Is that Old Norse, too?" Neil asks.

Looking up at a corner of the room, where an old Sesame Street border is wrinkled, I say, "Germanic. It means all-ruler."

"Alaric, Alaric," Neil mutters. "Gilly, it's Mr. Allenby!"

She pokes him and says, "Ta-da!"

"I have wandered far and wide," Alaric said, "but I've never seen such a cheery home."

William shrugged. "We're content, but it's been years since we were cheery."

Alison explained: "We never hunger or thirst or want for friends. But they have children to delight them now and care for them in years to come. We do not." She began to weep.

"We had a son once," William said. "A handsome boy. So bright."

"Gee, thanks," Neil says.

"What happened to him?" Alaric asked.

"I made an unwitting pact with the wind," William said. "I believe that Nigel will come back to us as a knight. My fair wife is

.

not so sure. 'Who knows when?' she asks. 'Or even why?' In the meantime, our house is empty of laughter." While Alison wiped at her tears, William described how Nigel had been spirited away.

Alaric pretended to be amazed. "Sailors call such creatures dolphins," he said. "Don't worry. They'll take good care of your son." He moved his chair to the window so he could breathe the salt air. "How the sea changes," he mused. "Calm one moment, stormy the next. My ship sank many leagues west of here, near the Dark Isle of Glandis. I should have been dashed onto its rocky shore, but the currents brought me to you. By some miracle."

William and Alison leaned forward. They listened closely while Alaric spoke:

"Glandis is ruled by the good Queen Morna."

"Good Queen Lorna?" Gillian asks.

"Morna. By the way," I ask, twisting one last time, "what does P-I-T-B mean?"

I turn back while Gillian answers, "Pain in the Butt." She giggles.

"Lorna's just kidding," Neil says.

"We know that," I tell Gillian.

She nods to Mr. Allenby.

"Morna's name means 'beloved,'" Alaric said. "Just before her husband, the king, died, she bore him a lovely daughter. The girl's name is Fiona—"

"As in Leona," Neil tells Gillian. Leona is Jerry and Regan's girl. She's Neil's age but prefers looking after Gillian when the three of them go to the park. Leona helps Gillian hold the string of Neil's kite.

"We like Leona," Gillian tells Mr. Allenby. "We like Fiona, too. She's the Princess of Glandis!"

"Fiona's name means 'the white one,'" Alaric said. "Alas, a plague swept the island and the king fell incurably ill. On his deathbed, he bound Morna to a promise. So that no child in the realm would be exalted above Fiona, the queen should never marry again. Morna agreed. Yet barely a month after he died, she fell in love with a handsome lord from a distant kingdom. Who could blame her? She was still young. She and her lord spent hours walking in orchards or listening to minstrels singing ballads of love. But though he often asked her to marry him, she refused. At last he demanded that she marry him, and she told him to leave. Enraged, he revealed his true form. He was a sorcerer."

"All right!" Neil exclaims.

"He had disguised himself in the hope of stealing her crown. Only her undying love for the king had saved her. But, now, the sorcerer cast a spell."

"What was it?" Alison asked.

"We must speak of it in whispers," Alaric said. "Dark clouds cover the island so the sun can never shine on it. Crops can barely grow. Storms batter ships from kingdoms that try to send food. The people are sick and weak. Even now, four years after he cast the spell, the sorcerer hopes for victory. He thinks Morna will surrender her crown rather than watch her people suffer as they do."

"Why doesn't she surrender it?" William asked. "Is she as stubborn as her enemy is evil?"

"Morna is proud, not stubborn!" Alaric pointed a bony finger and narrowed his eyes. "Speak no ill of a queen whose people are cowards. All they do is pray for a champion to deliver them. She refuses to bow to the sorcerer because she has true hope. I will tell you why." Suddenly, the wind blew afresh, and Alaric rose. "I must go," he said.

"Forgive me for angering you," William cried. "Stay and finish your tale."

Alaric shook his head. "I leave in haste, not anger. When the tide ebbs, I cannot sit still. I should ask your pardon for I carry no gold to repay your hospitality. Seven days and seven nights, you let me sleep on your feather mattress while you slept on straw. For each day and night shall I send you one gift. On the eighth day you shared your food with me and listened to an old man's tale. For this day you deserve a special gift. Goodbye, my friends. May tears never again flow within these walls."

Before William or Alison could speak, Alaric left. They ran outside and called his name but the darkness had swallowed him. The tide had washed his footprints from the sand.

Gillian seems to be fast asleep. I should know better. Even as I rise from the edge of her bed, she mumbles, "Don't stop." I sit down and continue. It's getting late, but she'll like this part. So will Neil, though he'll pretend otherwise.

Weeks passed. William often thought of Glandis. "The people are waiting for someone to deliver them," he told Alison. "Were I ten years younger, I'd sail to the island to try my hand against the sorcerer—myself."

She laughed kindly at his fancies. "Glory is for knights," she said. "Fishermen may only dream. And little boys."

"And little girls," I say, stroking Gillian's hair.

"And elephants," she adds. "Did you know that Mr. Allenby doesn't dream in living colour?"

"What does he dream in?"

"Cartoons, of course."

"Of course."

"Gee, Dad," Neil says. "Now I know where you get your imagination."

"Thank you, son. Thank you, oh light of my life."

.

46

"Yeah, yeah," he says.

One morning, while William mended his nets, he saw a faraway ship. It sailed swiftly toward him as if borne by wings. Although it looked like a ship, he soon saw that it was smaller than his boat. A green sail with silver stripes billowed from a mast no taller than a man. The figurehead was a dolphin. He called for Alison, and she came from the garden. They both watched while invisible hands loosed the sails.

"Ahoy!" William called.

No one answered. Bobbing like a gull, the little ship came to rest. He waded into the water and, grasping the rope under the prow, he pulled the ship ashore. Then he and Alison peered over the gunwale. Eight babies slept on the deck. Each was swaddled in a blanket of a different colour.

Unable to believe his eyes, William said, "Alaric's eight gifts!"

"Babies!" Gillian exclaims. "Did you hear that, Mr. Allenby?"

William and Alison carried the babies, two by two, into the cottage. They lay them in a row on the feather mattress. "Imagine, eight boys!" he exclaimed. "One might have consoled us for losing Nigel. Eight will bring us eight times the joy." Smiling, he removed the red blanket that kept the first child warm. William's smile vanished. The boy's hands were too large for his arms.

"Oh, no," Gillian says.

"Bet he's a handful," Neil adds.

Alison removed the orange blanket that kept the second child warm. This boy's legs were too long for his body.

Gillian, again: "Oh, no."

"It's a jest!" William cried. "I'd rather have one perfect child than eight such monsters!"

"Don't speak like that," Alison said, "or we'll lose them, too.

•

The gods never make a strange creature without endowing it with some talent. Let's see the rest of them."

Always hoping the next baby would be perfect, William watched her remove each one from its swaddling clothes.

The third boy was wrapped in a yellow blanket. His right arm was twice as thick as his left.

"Oh, no!" Gillian, who else?

The fourth boy, in green, had eyes too large for his head.

"Oh, no!" Neil, this time.

The fifth boy, in blue, had a chest that was twice as broad as his brothers'.

Gillian's "Oh, no!" is lost in Neil's, "Fifteen men on a dead man's chest! Yo-ho-ho and a bottle of rum!"

The sixth boy, in indigo, had hefty thighs and large feet.

Neil, his voice high-pitched: "Oh, no!"

And the seventh boy, in violet, had a huge, round belly.

Gillian and Neil, together: "Oh, no!"

How can I not laugh? They're such fine children. Both, together, the light of my life.

Alison reached for the eighth child, wrapped in white. "Let's see what's wrong with this boy," she said. When she removed the blanket, William laughed for joy. The eighth child was a girl, perfect in every way. Alison hugged her close. "Now I have the daughter I've longed for! To a father goes the privilege of naming his son—his sons—but a mother names her daughter. I'll call her Lilian, for her clothes are as white as the lily."

Gillian tells her elephant, "There I am!"

After helping Alison light a fire, William left the cottage. He finished mending his nets and put to sea. The little ship had left the shore. Steered by invisible hands, it had sailed away. He wondered, "Have we been punished or rewarded? Alaric said he would reward us. Alison must be right. The gods never make a strange creature without endowing it with some talent." And so, all that day, he tried to think of names for his new sons; yet none came to him. "Clearly they're special," he said, "and so should have special names." At dusk, he returned to shore. While he unloaded his boat, the wind called:

"Will-i-am."

"There's that wind again," Neil says.

William stopped working and heard these words:
With wrists like the yew, supple and strong,
Raedwald the Red a leader will be;
On legs bearing him swiftly like wings,
Oswald the Orange may easily flee;

Blessed with an arm as thick as the oak,
Edward the Yellow flings spears to their mark;
Only with falcon-sight, keen in the fray
Can Godwin the Green find light in the dark;

Diving more deeply than warm-blooded dolphins,
Baldwin the Blue will conquer the deep;
Higher than eagles could ever ascend,
Indigo Ivor will daringly leap;

Steadfast as cliffrock, battered by waves,
Violet Wystan will never give ground;
Yet in their one sister, so perfect, so pure
Will none of the seven boys' talents be found.

"Hey, Gilly," Neil says. "Dad's a poet and he doesn't know it. But his feet do." He waits until she faces him. Then he adds, "They're Longfellows!"

"I don't get it," she says.

"That's one of Uncle Jerry's jokes," I say. "From the days when he sold shoes."

"Oh," she says. Then she laughs.

Mr. Allenby seems unimpressed.

William ran to the cottage and recited the words to Alison.

"These aren't ordinary names," she said, "but our sons aren't ordinary boys." She picked up each one, kissed his brow, and said his name: "Raedwald, Oswald, Edward, Godwin, Baldwin, Ivor, and Wystan. Each is fit to become a knight. Perhaps, one day, people will say, 'There ride the sons of William Bowman!'"

"And of Alison Fair," he said. He picked up their daughter. "Lilian will ride in a carriage fit for a queen." They laughed, then looked out the window at the sea.

"Alaric has returned our happiness," Alison said. "Perhaps one day he will find Nigel and bring him back to us."

"Then," William added, "if the gods are willing, we'll live happily ever after!"

I kiss Gillian's brow and rise from her bed.

Neil asks, "Isn't it a bit early for that line?"

"Like I said," I tell him, "it's a long story." I turn off the lamp next to her bed. "Night, night, my sweet."

"Night, night, Daddy."

"Night, Mr. Allenby," Neil says. He steps back into the hall. After I pull the door half closed, we head for the family room. There we'll read till Alice comes home. She's giving a guest lecture at the School for Human Justice. It's to mark her recent appointment as a Queen's Counsel; of her

taking the silk. "By the way," I ask Neil, "I assume you're ready for your science test?"

Despite my concern, he says what I half expect him to say: "I'm always ready." And I say what he fully expects me to say: "Don't get cocky, son."

Even as we descend the few steps into the family room, he tries to change the subject. "So, what happens after Alaric sends the eight babies?"

"Nice try," I tell him. "You'll just have to wait."

And he, pretending to be Gillian's age, whines, "Aw, Dad!"

·

3

The Duke of Castle Fen

Neil has decided to join us tonight. He sits on the carpet with his back against Gillian's night table. I sit on the edge of the bed. While telling her the story, I can glance at Neil without having to twist. Mr. Allenby, the elephant, is all ears.

"So," I remind our children, "William and Alison now have seven sons and a daughter."

At first people laughed at the boys. "Such freaks!" the men agreed at the inn.

"I hope William brings them to the fair," one man said. "I'd gladly pay a penny to watch them dance."

Another said, "They should have been named for birds. The long-legged one could be Oswald the Stork, and the one who stares could be Godwin the Owl."

"Or animals," a third man said. "The ugliest boy is Ivor. He bounces from place to place like a frog. Perhaps he's a prince in disguise!"

"They're not very nice," Neil says.

"No," Gillian agrees. She tells Mr. Allenby, "They're just like those awful boys who make fun of Neil."

"What awful boys?" I ask him.

"It doesn't matter," he mumbles.

I say, "I see," though I don't.

•

He looks relieved.

Before long, the people stopped laughing at the seven boys for they began working as soon as they learned to walk. Oswald ran errands on his long legs. Ivor caught birds by leaping into the air and dropping baskets on them from above. Raedwald used his powerful hands to bend iron bands into barrel hoops. While Baldwin kept a fire bright by blowing on the flames, strong-armed Edward wrought tools on an anvil. And Wystan, whose belly was solid muscle, could lift as much as any grown man.

William wanted to love his sons equally, but he grew fondest of Godwin. This boy, who always wore green, became both a fisherman and a huntsman. With his keen eyes, he could spot fish far beneath the waves and knew exactly where to drop his nets. He also became a skillful archer and helped William hunt.

While the men laughed at the boys, the women praised Lilian.

Gillian grins toward Neil.

"She's the prettiest girl on the coast," the women agreed. But even as the men stopped their laughing, the women began shaking their heads. "Lilian may be pretty," they agreed, "but she's of no help to her mother in the house."

"Instead of sewing proper seams," one woman said, "she sews them as crooked as our coastline!"

"Instead of sweeping sand out of the cottage," said another, "I've heard she sweeps it in!"

"And instead of baking cakes all the same shape," a third woman cried, "she makes them as different as snowflakes!"

"I like snowflakes!" Gillian insists.

"I do, too," I say.

Neither the villagers nor Lilian's new parents understood why a child so beautiful seemed to have no talents. "Who will marry a girl who can't keep house?" William asked Alison. Still, they loved Lilian dearly.

At last Alison told her, "Never mind working, dear. Play on the shore and talk to the gulls."

Neil softly shrieks, "Ee-ee!" He tucks his hands into his armpits and flaps his folded arms.

"Don't mind him," Gillian tells Mr. Allenby.

When the boys entered their seventh year, Alison told William, "We should offer their services to the duke."

William laughed. Then he remembered his dream of raising a son to become a knight. He went to Castle Fen the very next day. Cap in hand, he stood in the midst of Gerald's great hall and asked him to accept the boys into his household.

Gerald laughed so hard, his face turned purple. "Ale!" he gasped, even as he choked.

Gillian and Neil also laugh. "That's Uncle Jerry, all right," Neil says. "He's fond of his cups."

"Where did you hear that?" I ask.

"Coming back from the acreage, last month. You told Mom, 'Jerry's fond of his cups, all right.' You thought we were both asleep—it was so late."

"Did I, now?"

"And Mom said, 'Don't be so …'" His frown turns into a grin even as a voice behind me announces, "Archaic."

I twist to find Alice standing in the hall. She's holding a plastic laundry tub full of my shirts.

"Mommy's here!" Gillian tells Mr. Allenby. "Daddy's telling us a story," she tells her mother.

"And you're in it," Neil says. "You do all the housework—"

Alice pretends to glare at me. "Don't let me interrupt." She heads for our room to hang up my shirts. If I want them ironed, I do it myself. Good thing they're permanent press.

Untwisting, I ask, "Where were we?"

"The duke is in his cups," Neil says.

To which Gillian adds, "The queen was in the par-ler, eat-ing bread an' hunny!"

While the duke drank, William looked about. The hall was hung with tapestries to keep out the chill. Above the hall rose a wooden tower, and around the castle rose a high, stone wall. Still, he liked his cottage better than the castle. No tapestries hung on his walls, but they resounded with the laughter of children. Watching Gerald guzzle a flagon of ale, William thought, "How he's changed. He's grown so stout, he could eat an entire boar."

At last Gerald belched and wiped his mouth. "What a silly idea of yours!" he said. "Only the sons of other noblemen may serve here as pages. Go home."

"Wait, Brother," Megan said. "I've heard so much about these boys. They might make life more interesting for us."

Gerald downed a second flagon, rolled his eyes, and belched once more.

"Times of peace are so dull for you," Megan said. "Besides, seven boys can do much work, especially if they're as talented as I've heard."

"That's true," Gerald said at last. He told William, "Send them at once."

"And your daughter, too," Megan said. "I'll teach her how to read and write and wait on gentlewomen."

William frowned. "Even though Lilian's of no help at home," he thought, "Alison won't want to part with her. Still, I owe Lady Megan my thanks for swaying the duke." He agreed to do as she asked.

"That's Aunt Regan, all right," Neil announces. "Mom says she keeps Uncle Jerry on an even keel."

Alice startles me by asking, "When did I say that?" Something tells me she's leaning in Gillian's doorway, just as Neil was last night. With her arms crossed.

Looking at the Sesame Street border, I ask, "Would Mumsy like to join us?"

"No, Mumsy would not," she says. "I'm just passing by."

Gillian whispers to Mr. Allenby, "That's what Neil said, too."

It shouldn't surprise me but it does: how much children remember from day to day, even month to month.

The next seven years passed slowly for William and Alison. They saw their children only on feast days. Snow fell, then melted; trees blossomed, then dropped their leaves; birds flew south and returned to lay their eggs. Thirteen years after finding the children in the magical ship, William and Alison watched proudly while the duke presented each boy with silver spurs. All the courtiers cheered. William's dream that his sons should become more than fishermen had come true. No one would call them Raedwald the Cooper or Edward the Smith. They were now Squire Raedwald and Squire Edward.

"Hoo-ray!" Gillian cries.

"Hoo-ray," Neil says.

Alice claps softly.

I decide not to mention Nigel.

The duke grunted when he sat down. He arranged the folds of his cloak over his belly. "Today is a happy day for you," Gerald told William and Alison. "But it's a doubly happy day for me. You know I never remarried after my wife died. I found no one worthy

•

enough to wed. Now, I have. Bowman, I've decided to marry your daughter."

William looked at Lilian, who stood among the ladies-in-waiting. Her face turned paler than her white gown. When Gerald looked at her, she cried, "No!"

He scowled when she ran to Alison. He demanded, "You dare refuse a duke?"

Now Alison spoke. "Sire, would April make August a good bride? Lilian is young enough to be your daughter."

He struggled to his feet. "Oh, all right," he growled. "I'll wait till she's fifteen." He glared at William. "Well, does a woman run your house?"

The courtiers laughed.

"Um, Dad?" Neil says.

"Yes, son?"

"Uncle Jerry would never marry Gillian even if he was—"

"Huh?" Gillian asks. She frowns toward the doorway as though expecting her mother to explain.

Neil asks me, "Wouldn't that be incest?"

When Alice laughs softly, I turn on the bed and ask him, "Where do you learn such things?"

"I do go to school."

"To tell the truth," I say, "I'm not sure if it would be incest. My grandfather nearly married one of his nieces after he was widowed."

"That's different," Neil says. "Your family's … different."

When Alice chuckles, I look to her for help, but she's enjoying herself too much. "Just because I named the duke after Jerry," I tell Neil, "doesn't mean the duke is Jerry."

"But I'm Lilian," Gillian insists.

"Yes, my sweet."

"And Neil's Nigel," Gillian tells Alice. "I'm learning to read and write. Not Neil, though. He's just learning to be a knight." Gillian presses her ear to Mr. Allenby's trunk. Then she adds, "Nigel is."

"How nice," Alice says. "In shining armour?"

"Not yet," I say. "He's still a squire."

"Swimming around with all those dolphins," Neil adds.

"The Dolphin Liberation Front," Gillian declares.

At this Alice breaks into laughter. When I frown at her, she covers her mouth with her hands as if she's praying. She can't help herself. She turns from the doorway and heads for the family room. We can hear her laughing while she gasps, "The Dolphin Liberation Front!"

I turn my back to the door and pat Mr. Allenby's ear. "Don't listen to any of them," I say.

Gillian smiles. She likes it when I treat him like one of the family. Mind you, I put my foot down when it comes to buying him Christmas gifts. She claims he wants a Yamaha Clavinova because it can sound like a piano, an organ or a harpsichord.

William took a bold step forward. He said, "Lilian has no wish to marry you, duke or not. Her mother and I love her too much to force her into marriage. Sire, I've been your vassal for twenty years. I fought for you. It's true you gave me land, but my first duty is to my family." William held out the glove Gerald had given him as a token of their bond.

From the whiskers at his chin to the hair on his head, Gerald's face turned black with anger. "Wretch!" he roared. "Ungrateful—!"

William threw his glove at the duke's feet.

The courtiers gasped.

Bellowing like a wounded boar, Gerald tried to grasp Lilian's arm. Alison cried out. The seven boys formed a circle around their mother and sister.

"Traitors!" Gerald screamed. His face turned white with fear. He tried to draw his sword, but he could not reach across his belly for the hilt.

Not one courtier moved to help him.

William led his family from the great hall, and Gerald's words echoed through the castle:

"You'll pay for this!"

"Uh-oh," Neil says.

Gillian repeats, "Uh-oh."

Later that day, three friends of William and Alison visited the cottage. "We heard what happened," the eldest said. "We also heard that no one raised a hand to help the duke. The people are tired of him. We pledge the support of the village and the town in your coming battle."

William stopped his friend from kneeling. "There won't be a battle," he said. "I won't fight Gerald, and I ask no man to fight for me. If I'm brought before the court, I'll be proven innocent. The law says a nobleman cannot take a freeman's daughter. The king will surely name a wiser man as Duke of Castle Fen."

"If I were king," the second visitor said, "I would name you."

"Why wait?" the third visitor asked. "Defeat the duke, and we'll proclaim you our lord."

William cried, "No!" and backed away. "I fought to keep this land safe from those who would have plundered it. I'll never fight to take what belongs to another."

Dismayed, the three men left.

The family had just begun its evening meal when everyone heard the clatter of hooves and the rattle of armour. An armed man flung the door open, and Alison screamed.

"Oh, no!" Gillian cries. Then she tells Mr. Allenby, "Don't be scared."

Pretending he's Mr. Allenby, Neil says in a high-pitched voice, "I'm not scared."

Megan entered the cottage. "My brother has sent a messenger to the king," she said. "He charges you with planning a rebellion. It's all my fault. I should have sent Lilian home the first time Gerald looked at her. Please, forgive me." Then she ordered, "You must leave at once!"

William looked at Godwin, who stared back with his huge eyes. Then William shook his head. "We could never leave. This is our home."

"Yet I've heard you won't fight," Megan said. "The king long ago declared Rivermouth, north of here, a city of refuge. It's the one place in this land where vengeance cannot trample the law. You can hide there in safety."

"All our lives?" Alison asked. "How long would we be happy in a city? Is there no place we can be safe and happy, both?"

"Only one, Mother," Lilian said. She sat by the fireplace, where she saw the answer written in the flames.

Her brothers looked surprised that she had spoken. "Where?" Godwin asked.

Lilian replied, "The Dark Isle of Glandis."

"The Dark Isle of what?" Gillian asks.

"Glandis," Neil replies. "Where Alaric said things are in a pickle because the queen wouldn't marry that sorcerer."

"What kind of pickle?" Gillian asks.

"It's a figure of speech," I say.

"A what?"

Before I can explain, Neil says, "Interesting—how Lilian knows about the one place they can be safe and happy."

•

"She saw the answer in the flames," I say.

"That's right," Gillian tells him. "It's my story, and I see everything."

Imitating a fairy tale character—or, more likely, me—Neil says, "And how do you see these things, pray tell?" He asks this although we know what she will say: "Through Mr. Allenby."

4

The Voyage of the Reckless

WILLIAM HATED RIVERMOUTH. Narrow streets snaked among dingy houses; plucked feathers choked the gutters; dogs rooted for scraps. Masons hammered. Vendors hawked. Women haggled. Babies howled. The noise deafened him. He swore not to stay in the city a moment longer than he had to. Every day, he searched for passage to Glandis but no one would sail to the Dark Isle.

At last, an innkeeper told him about a trader named Avery Shipman. "For gold he would sail a bucket through a firestorm," the innkeeper said.

"Dad," Neil says. "We don't know anyone with a name like Avery."

"What? Oh," I say. "Well, um, what about Mr. Allenby?"

"But he's Alaric," Gillian cries.

"That's right, my sweet. He is. But can't he be another character, too?"

"Did you hear that?" she asks her elephant. "You're in this story twice!"

"Not bad for such a little guy," Neil says.

"He's not little," she tells him. "He's huge. If he didn't make himself small, he wouldn't be able to fit in my room."

"Sorry," Neil says. "I forgot about imagination running in this family."

"Ahem," I say.

The innkeeper told William, "Avery calls his ship the *Reckless*, and I'll tell you something between friends. I wouldn't trust him. Still, if you're set on your course, his room's upstairs."

William found Avery bent over charts. He had narrow eyes and a face like a rat's.

Gillian says, "Mr. Allenby doesn't have a face like a rat!"

"It's a figure of speech," Neil says.

"Oh."

When William explained what he wanted, Avery laughed until William said, "You could trade your goods on the isle for ten times their worth."

Avery's eyes lit up. Then he shrugged. "All your gold won't buy a voyage to Glandis," he said. "Where will I find a crew foolish enough to man my ship?"

"My sons," William offered.

"Well, then," Avery said, "she's at your service! Now, let's see your gold."

So began the westward voyage of the *Reckless*. She was a broad, single-masted ship with much space for cargo and little for passengers. Everyone slept on deck. The ship's real master was William because Avery did no work in spite of his name, Shipman. He lay about all day and spun tales of faraway lands.

"Just like Alaric!" Neil exclaims. "See, Gilly? That's why Mr. Allenby has to be Alaric and Avery. Good one, Dad."

In fact, I hadn't planned this, but once again I tell him, "Thank you, son. Thank you, oh light of my life."

This time it's Gillian who says, to Mr. Allenby, "Yeah, yeah."

One evening, instead of turning red and setting slowly, the sun went out like a snuffed candle. The sky in front of the *Reckless* turned as black as pitch.

·

"I see why," Godwin told the others. "There's a black cloud covering the horizon."

"We're halfway to the Dark Isle," Avery explained. "Soon the sun and stars will no longer light our way."

"You know much about foreign lands," Alison said. "Tell us why Queen Morna refuses to surrender her crown to the sorcerer."

Avery stretched out on deck and everyone except William gathered to listen. He remained at the steerboard. From here he heard the end of a tale begun long ago.

When Neil's eyes shift from me to the doorway, I guess that Alice has returned. Without twisting, I ask, "Just passing by?"

She doesn't reply, and Neil chuckles.

"Morna refuses to give in," Avery said, "because she knows there's a way to break every spell. The sorcerer was so sure he could win the crown that he provided the way himself. He created the five curses of the New Year. The curse of the first day is a dark knight on a dark horse."

"Ooh," Neil says.

"Ooh," Gillian repeats.

A ghostly voice echoes, "Ooh," and I say, "Thank you, Mumsy."

It's Alice's turn to chuckle.

"What's the curse of the second day?" Godwin asked.

"No one knows," Avery replied. "Each year, knights from around the world sail to the island. Many drown off its coast. None of those who've landed have defeated the dark knight, so no one has seen the curse of the second day. Each year, the people's hopes rise, only to sink further."

Alison recalled Alaric's words: "Yet Morna has true hope."

"Yes. One morning, while she walked on the shore, she heard

the wind call her name. It told her a riddle." In the eerie twilight, Avery chanted:

> To find the sun who hides from sight,
> Take heart, and with your shadows fight,
> For Glandis can never be truly free
> Till a rainbow curves from sky to sea.

"Is that s-u-n or s-o-n?" Gillian asks.

"In the riddle, you mean?" Neil says.

She nods without looking at him.

"Must be s-u-n," he replies. Then he says, "Don't worry, Dad. I'm not giving anything away."

"What are you giving away?" Gillian asks.

Neil and I both say, "Nothing!"

Alice chuckles again.

William scoffed at Avery, then asked, "How can there be a rainbow if there's no sun in the sky?"

"And how can anyone fight their shadows," Alison asked, "if there's no sun to cast them?"

"Good one, Mom," Neil tells Alice.

Avery shrugged. "It's nothing to me. Morna must think there's an answer. She ordered masons to carve the riddle into the face of a cliff beneath her castle. If she can't find the answer, she'll have to find knights valiant enough to defeat the five curses. She has even decreed that the man who frees the island will marry her daughter and, one day, become Prince of Glandis." Avery laughed. "My father taught me how to use a bow and arrow, but I'm no warrior!"

"So, your father was an archer?" William asked.

Avery nodded proudly, and William looked at him in a new light.

·

"Speaking of lights," Alice says from behind me. "It's time this little girl's light was out."

"Aw, Mom!" Neil says.

Gillian adds a drawn-out, "I'm not sleep-y."

"I'll bet Mr. Allenby is, though," her mother insists.

Without turning, I tell her, "I'm nearly done."

"Plus we're getting to the good part," Neil adds.

"How would you know?" I ask.

"Because," he says.

The next day, the sun set in late afternoon. The day after, at noon. The sky in the east remained clear while the sky in the west looked dark. The Reckless sailed into churning seas. William awoke at dawn to the sound of waves breaking onto rocks. He searched astern for the rising sun and saw nothing. Clouds filled the entire sky. Dead ahead loomed jagged cliffs.

Alison rose and whispered, "So this will be our new home."

While the *Reckless* neared the island, the wind blew more strongly. It tore at the sail and flung waves to batter the ship. Both William and Wystan had to hold the steerboard now. Rain drenched everyone. Lightning flashed. Thunder boomed.

"Uh-oh," Gillian tells Mr. Allenby.

"Uh-oh," Neil adds. After he looks at Alice, she adds:

"Uh-oh."

Avery clawed his way up the tilted deck to the stern. He yelled above the wind, "Go about! We must approach the island from another tack!"

William shouted, "Not till Alison and the children have tied themselves down! Otherwise, they'll be swept overboard as soon as we change course. Wystan, help the others!"

The boy with the huge belly obeyed, but Avery refused to take orders from anyone. He lunged for the steerboard and knocked William off his feet. "My cargo is more precious than your family!" Avery cried.

Pitching and rolling, the *Reckless* turned broadside to the wind. When the first wave struck, the port gunwale dipped under water. William grabbed a rope to keep from tumbling overboard. Alison and the boys wedged themselves among bales of cargo. Only Lilian stood tall.

"Tie yourself down!" William yelled.

Lilian did not hear him. She faced the wind. It whipped at her white cloak and her long, black hair. She raised her arms and spoke words he could not hear.

The second wave smashed a hole in the hull. The *Reckless* capsized. William and Alison, Lilian, the boys and Avery—all of them tumbled into the sea. The ship jolted, then jolted again. It crashed against rocks. William heard two sounds before a beam struck his head: first, Alison's cries; then, the groans of the *Reckless* while she broke in two and sank.

"Right," Alice says, entering the room, "that's it for tonight."

"Aw, Mom!" Neil says, but he rises from the floor.

"Aw," Gillian tells her elephant.

I brush the dark hair off her brow and kiss her. "Night, night, my sweet."

"Not yet," she insists, shaking her head.

Alice waits until we head for the door. Then she bends to kiss Gillian and says, "Night, night, sweetie."

Gillian shakes her head once more. "Know what Mr. Allenby wants?" She crooks a finger at Alice, who bends so Gillian can whisper.

Moving from the doorway, Neil and I call, "Night, Mr. Allenby," but Alice turns and says, "Not just yet. We'll meet you downstairs."

•

Neil and I walk together along the hall, then down the few steps into the family room. "Now, that's what you call a cliffhanger," he says. Glancing over his shoulder, he adds, "TV, probably."

"I'm not so sure," I say. I take my place and he takes his, though he doesn't lie down — in case Gillian wants the other half of the love seat. We sit like this. We listen and watch.

First we hear Alice ask, "Don't you want your robe?"

Then we hear Gillian's reply: "Just Mr. Allenby." Not that Alice has to be told. Gillian doesn't go anywhere in the house without Mr. Allenby. We see her approach us along the hall. Alice follows. Gillian holds her elephant in front of her, with her left hand, so she can see where she's going. She stops when Alice warns, "The stairs."

"We knew that," Gillian tells Mr. Allenby. With her free hand, her right hand, she clasps the railing and makes her way down, one step at a time.

I don't know how many times I've sat here watching her do this, hoping to catch her if she falls. She never does.

Alice waits at the top until Gillian reaches the bottom. When Gillian turns toward her piano, Alice also makes her way down. She settles in her favourite chair while Gillian approaches her piano bench. I never move it except to dust. It stands in the exact, right spot so that Gillian can find it, always find her place on the edge of this bench. She reaches for the keyboard with her right hand, satisfies herself she's in the centre, and puts Mr. Allenby down. His spot on the bench is to her left, within easy reach. Then, pedalling, she plays.

She is learning the Adagio sostenuto, the first movement of Beethoven's Sonata Quasi una Fantasia. His Moonlight Sonata. She has learned it — three lines at a time, one page a month — by listening to her teacher; by listening to it on disc. The piece is in C sharp minor. It is elegaic, hardly a piece for someone so young, and yet she practises the square-cornered displacement—used for rapid shifts—and a motion called, of all things, the fictive legato. This one requires courage, the courage to throw her hand from one position to the next. And so she lifts her hands high, she flings them to the right or left and, once she has learned a piece, she can find any note, any chord she wants.

At the end of the movement she waits for that final chord to die away. Without acknowledging our faint applause, she says, "Night, Mommy." Then, with Mr. Allenby once more guiding her way, Gillian returns to bed.

We sit here, the three of us, feeling helpless. And yet we remind ourselves that we're no more helpless than Gillian; that there's only so much we can do for her. Only so much that she, though a mere child of eight, expects from us. At last, Alice picks up her book, Susan Quinn's biography of Marie Curie. I pick up the book I started months ago. It's Albrecht Fölsing's biography of Albert Einstein. Neil stretches out on the love seat from which he and Gillian watch TV. He goes back to reading his own book. It's a commemorative edition of Treasure Island, illustrated by N.C. Wyeth, a gift from my younger sister.

"Speaking of suspense," I ask, "what about those awful boys?"

"What awful boys?" he asks. But when Alice looks at him, he sighs. "We were talking about multiculturalism in current events," he says. "About real names. That's when the kids found out my full name."

"How?" Alice asks.

"From Mrs. Mcaulay. She didn't mean anything by it. But she asked me to spell it out and she wrote it on the board along with some other names. You know, like Ming and Tololwa. And when I was walking Gilly home from her school, some guys from my class yelled, 'Sunil! Sunil!' Only they pronounced it Sue-Neil."

"Oh," I say. "I'm sorry."

He shrugs. "I only got mad when Gilly started crying."

·

"Why would Gillian do that?" Alice asks. He refuses to answer but she keeps her eyes on him until he has to reply.

He shrugs again. "They started yelling, 'Neil's a Paki! Neil's a Paki!' Gilly didn't know what was going on. But she knew it wasn't nice. That's what she meant by awful boys. They're not awful. They're just stupid. Well, some of them are."

"And what did you do?" I ask. No—I demand. I can feel my pulse racing the way it used to, years ago, when the same thing happened to me. But in those days, the awful boys had a wider vocabulary that included Brownie and Nigger.

Alice gives me a worried look, as if I'll grow angry, but the time for anger has passed. For me, at least.

Neil opens his book. "I yelled back, 'My mom was born here. My dad was born in India. That makes me only half a Paki.'"

I start laughing. I can't help it—he can be such a delight. I laugh so long and so hard that Alice glares at me. Clearly, she doesn't share my feelings about what happened. Knowing her, she'll be on the phone to Neil's principal first thing tomorrow. His name is Thomas Babington. Isn't it odd? Here she is, a lawyer by training—a practitioner of the world's most cynical art—and yet she expects far more justice in this life than I ever would. "Half a Paki!" I sputter, and she says, sharply, "Vikram, stop it!"

"Vikram," Neil mutters. Then, "Hey!" He swivels into a sitting position with Treasure Island clutched to his chest. "You're William!" he cries.

"Guilty," I admit.

"Then who's the real hero of this story? Is it Nigel, who Alaric's training for knighthood—"

"Whom," I say.

"Or is it William, who thinks his fighting days are over?"

"I told you," I remind him. "It's Gillian-Lilian. She's special." Alice

•

70

looks at me fondly now, but neither of us is prepared for what comes next.

Neil stretches out once more, takes up his book, and announces, "You got that right." Lying down like this, he can't see the tears welling in his mother's eyes. She long ago stopped trying to hide it from me—that deep, maternal sorrow my stories can't hope to dispel.

·

5

Castle Gloom

ALICE HAS ALSO DECIDED to join us, but Gillian's room feels cozy, not crowded. It's a neatly kept room, with a place for everything, everything in its place. As before, Neil sits on the carpet with his back against Gillian's night table. I sit on the edge of the bed. Alice, too, sits on the carpet. She keeps adjusting the cushion wedged between the small of her back and Gillian's chest of drawers. With the whole family listening, the story will take longer to tell, so we've gathered earlier than usual.

"Alors," I announce, "the Reckless has sunk off the coast of Glandis."

"Don't be scared," Gillian tells Mr. Allenby. "They didn't drown."

"They must be tired of treading water, though," Neil says. When I look at him, he explains with a straight face, "It's been a night and a day since the ship sank."

Nodding, Alice smiles knowingly. She's reminding me that, around children, a body has to be quick on his feet.

When he awoke, William found himself lying face down on a sandy beach. It stretched before him toward a cliff. Turning onto his back, he saw the boys looking down at him. Alison and Lilian were also safe. He rose and hugged them, then counted his sons to make sure they numbered seven. He did this twice. Then he asked, "Where's Avery?"

Everyone looked about.

•

"There!" Godwin said. "Trapped in the shoals. He's drowning."

"Oops," Neil says.

William ran toward the murky sea. Avery's head was barely above water. "Baldwin," William shouted, "we must save him!"

"He nearly killed us!" Alison cried.

"The gods saved us," William called back. "I must repay our debt." After plunging into the surf, he and his barrel-chested son swam toward the shoals. Baldwin reached Avery first. He held the trader's head above water until William could pull Avery's limp body onto his back. All three swept ashore like driftwood.

After opening his eyes, Avery asked, "Where am I? It's so gloomy." He looked like a frightened, half-drowned rat. "Am I in the next world?"

"There's that rat again," Neil says.

"You're in Glandis," William replied. "You could have killed us all. Since I saved your life, you're my servant till I set you free."

Laughing, Avery told the clouds, "I've lost a ship and gained a master!" He tried to rise, but his knees buckled. "I need rest," he moaned.

"Father," Godwin called, "I see a castle on top of this cliff. And town walls."

"Godwin has huge eyes," Gillian tells Alice. "And he always wears green."

"I see," Alice says.

William grasped Avery's collar and dragged him to his feet. "Let's see how hospitable these islanders are," William said.

Using his keen eyes, Godwin led his family along a path up the cliff face. When they passed the riddle carved in stone, they could barely make out its words. A faint glow marked the spot where the sun hid from sight. Soon they entered the town. Not one person bade them welcome. Gaunt figures, skulking through the fog, barely glanced at the newcomers. Wooden houses leaned against one another because their timbers had warped. Rusted, iron fences ringed gardens overgrown with weeds. The streets needed recobbling.

"I hated Rivermouth for smelling so vile," William told Alison, "but it felt full of life. This town might just as well be a graveyard."

She tightened her arm around Lilian's shoulder. "Everything is grey, brown or black," Alison said. "We might never see green fields again, but at least we're safe. All we have to do is find a place to sleep."

At last, on one side of the town square, they found what looked like an inn. After William knocked, a thin man in loosely fitting clothes opened the door. Its hinges creaked.

"What do you want?" the man growled.

"We're strangers here," William said. "Can you give us food and shelter in return for work?"

"We have trouble enough sheltering our own people!" the man said. "As for food, only vultures eat in Glandis."

"Good one, Dad," Neil says.

The man pointed at the castle. "Ask the queen, who brought this on us. Ask her why she won't surrender her crown to the sorcerer. At least he wouldn't let us starve!" The innkeeper slammed the door in William's face.

"Not very nice," Gillian tells Mr. Allenby.

William sighed. With a heart as heavy as his step, he led the way to the castle. Its towers had crumbled. Ivy wound across its battlements. He walked boldly through an empty guardhouse and over a moat choked with rushes. The drawbridge chains, rusted and broken, clanked against moss-covered stone. Once past the castle walls, he saw two sentries huddled over a fire.

One of them called, "Who goes there?"

"William Bowman. I wish to see the queen. Why is the guardhouse unguarded?"

The sentry laughed with scorn. "Who would attack us?" he said. "Once we called this Castle Bold. Now it's Castle Gloom. Follow me."

William and his household walked through drafty hallways into a large room that was feebly lit by candles. Moth-eaten tapestries kept out neither the dampness nor the chill.

Queen Morna of Glandis slouched on her throne.

"Lorna doesn't slouch," Neil says.

"Mommy," Gillian calls to Alice, "did you know everyone in this story's from real life?"

"Somehow I got that impression," Alice says.

"When you were passing by?" I ask.

"Babysitters never slouch," Gillian tells Mr. Allenby. "It's like Neil says."

"What does Neil say?" I ask.

"Nothing!" he cries.

Gillian giggles. "One time Lorna made him do homework instead of watching a playoff game. He said, 'She's so stiff, she has a poker up her—'"

At once, I say, "Neil!" and he says, "I never did!"

"Where does your son get such ideas?" I ask Alice.

"I haven't a clue," she says.

Wrapped in a faded, scarlet cloak, Morna soaked her feet in a bucket of steaming water. A tattered nightcap poked through the top of her tarnished crown. She held a slice of black bread with one hand and a pint of ale with the other. Next to her, at a small table, sat her daughter, Princess Fiona. The princess wore a fur-trimmed robe, and her long, blonde hair fell loosely from under a velvet cap. Her blue eyes outshone the sapphires at her throat. In front of her lay a platter of roast fowl, a bowl of fruit, and a goblet of wine.

Even as the sentry presented William, Morna sneezed. "Welcome to Glandis," she declared. "Hurry back to your fire," she told the sentry. Then she asked William, "What ill wind blows you here?"

He told her about Gerald's accusation of treason. "Knowing I defied a duke," William asked, "can you accept us as subjects?"

"Of course!" she said.

The earl marshall stepped out of shadows behind her throne. "Your Majesty," he warned, "if you accept this man as your vassal, you'll become responsible for his deeds—present and past. That's the law."

"True," she said. "Perhaps you should summon the council."

The earl marshall left the room. Moments later, he returned with twelve knights. They coughed and sniffed. One hobbled on a cane because his joints had stiffened from the dampness. Another squinted through the gloom. A third was so thin, his bones rattled in his armour.

"And his teeth rattled in his head," Neil suggests.

"No, they didn't," I say, "but thank you for that."

The queen explained her dilemma. After the knights muttered among themselves, the eldest spoke: "Your Majesty," he said, "we must agree with the earl marshall. What if the Duke of Castle Fen followed this Bowman? Would you defend a man you barely know?"

•

"The duke won't risk drowning to come here," Morna said. "Besides, we need strong, healthy subjects like him. And his servant. His sons are strange, but they look so cheerful! I thank you for your advice but I think I'll do as I please."

The old knight bowed while saying, "Your Majesty is well known for doing as she pleases."

"I welcome you, Bowman," she declared. "I can make you my vassal, but I can't give you land. I thus owe you a boon, which you may claim at any time."

Neil tells Alice, "The average North American child wouldn't understand what a boon is."

"Oh, really?" she says.

"But we're not average North American children," Gillian adds.

Alice looks surprised, then shakes her head. She should know by now—though we both tend to forget—that nothing children say should surprise us.

"I don't know where you'll live," Morna told William, "but for tonight you can stay here."

"I ask for nothing more," William said. "My sons may be squires, but they can still work with their hands."

"Well then," she said, "in the morning, you can repair to the town. Then you can repair it."

I pause, but no one laughs at Morna's jest.

"What good is land in this kingdom?" she mused. "A bushel of weeds grows for every peck of grain." She slammed her fist on the arm of her throne. "But Fiona must eat well, for I've promised her hand to the champion who frees us."

Looking at the princess reminded Alison of Nigel. "He would be about her age now," Alison thought. She told Morna, "Our daughter, Lilian, can read and sing. Are there any gentlewomen in the castle she could serve?"

"Yes, my wife! Mine!" said the Knights of Glandis.

Fiona pouted. "Mother," she said, "none of my ladies-in-waiting know any new stories or songs. This girl might make a fine companion."

"So be it," Morna ordered. "Bring black bread and soup for my guests. Bring ale for my knights. Bring white bread and wine for Lady Lilian." Morna rubbed her hands over a candle flame. "What a day this has turned out to be! For the first time in years, I have new subjects."

"Fiona even sounds like Leona," Neil says. He tells his mother, "Aunt Regan said that when Fiona was little, she'd change her clothes three, four times a day. A real princess, all right."

"What's wrong with that?" Gillian asks.

"Nothing, dear," Alice says. "Neil's just being judgemental. Like his father."

Neil and I both say, "I am not!"

When Alice scoffs, so does Gillian. "Right," she says, as her mother often does. "Right."

"Humph," Neil adds. Then, "Gilly! Want to hear a joke?"

She turns from Alice to him.

"What do you call a camel with a straight back?"

Gillian frowns.

"Humphrey!" he exclaims. He looks delighted when she laughs.

"Did you get that?" she asks Mr. Allenby. "Hump-free." With one hand she makes him nod. His trunk flops on her blanket.

I wait patiently and, for a while, it seems there will be no more interruptions. I should know better.

And so, William and Alison with their children and servant settled on the Dark Isle of Glandis. At first the islanders treated them coldly, but the family soon set about earning its keep. Baldwin and Edward became blacksmiths. They forged new tools, new chains, new plows—to replace those that had rusted.

"Edward has a huge right arm," Neil tells Alice. "And he always wears yellow."

She nods her thanks.

"Say, Dad," he says. "Shouldn't his name be Yedward?"

Trying to sound innocent, I ask, "Why?"

"You know," he says. "Because of Roy G. Biv."

"Who's Roy G. Biv?" Gillian asks.

"Those are the colours of the—"

"Not yet," I say.

But he can't let it go. He casually asks, "Say, Dad, what's an acronym?"

"Who's Anakronim?" Gillian asks.

"Never mind," I tell her. "Your brother's just showing off."

"Humph," Neil says. "Better an acronym than an anachronism."

Alice laughs and laughs—she can't help herself. "See what you've done?" she says, looking at me. "That's what you get for teaching him how to do the cryptic crossword."

This time, when Neil says, "Say, Dad," I exclaim, "Please!" Then I mutter, "Where was I?" but no one comes to my rescue. "Oh, yes."

Swinging an axe with each hand, Raedwald cleared trails through overgrown brush.

"He has huge hands," Gillian tells Alice. "And he always wears red."

"I see," Alice says.

Ivor leapt into treetops to fell the driest branches, and Avery carted them away for firewood.

"Ivor's the one who looks like a frog," Gillian explains. "He wears indigo. He bounces from place to place. Boing, boing—"

"Boing," her mother adds.

Keen-eyed Godwin became a guide for people afraid of losing their way. Long-legged Oswald ran errands. Wystan also hurried to and fro. He moved wagons stuck in mud. He supported rafters on his shoulders while William replaced rotting posts. Wystan even pulled the newly-forged plows through stony fields.

Gillian says, "Wystan has, um?"

"A huge, round belly," Nigel reminds her.

"We knew that," she tells Mr. Allenby. "He always wears violet."

"But," Neil adds, grinning at me, "his name should be Vystan." Neil puts on a Swedish accent he learned from watching The Muppet Show with Gillian. "Yoo-hoo, Vys-tan!"

Alice laughs again, this time at my impatience. She makes a face to remind me not to take all this too seriously. I'm not. I'm just losing my place. Still, I do laugh at myself at last, and she looks pleased.

Although William had no land, the townspeople treated him with respect. The glimpse of a red or green or violet cloak became a welcome sight to people who lived in eternal gloom. But not everyone smiled at him. One day he met the innkeeper in the town square.

"Just because you have special sons," the man said, "don't think you're better than us."

"What do you mean?" William asked.

The innkeeper sneered. "Have you forgotten the five curses? The black knight will triumph once again, and your sons won't work so hard or so cheerfully after that. They'll learn there's nothing to work for. Just wait."

"Yes," Gillian tells Mr. Allenby. "Just wait."

"Are we at the end of a chapter?" Neil asks me. After I nod, he says, "Is this supposed to be an allegory?"

"What's analagory?" Gillian asks.

"No," I say. "Why?"

"Neil," Alice says, "your sister asked you a question."

He tells Gillian, "Sorry. That's where a story means something else. Right?" he asks me.

I wag my head in that Indian way I never knew I had until Alice pointed it out. The wag means maybe yes, maybe no.

"I think," Alice says, "strictly speaking, in an allegory there's a one-to-one correspondence between the fictional characters and real life. Maybe even between fictional situations and real life."

"Like Animal Farm," Neil tells Gillian.

"We don't know that one," she tells Mr. Allenby.

"Gulliver's Travels, then," he tells her. "You know, the Yahoos and the Houyhnhnms."

"The what?" she asks.

"The Yahoos look human but they act like animals," he says. "They're brutes. And the Houyhnhnms"—he drags this into a whinny—"look like horses but they reason like human beings."

"Oh, brother," I mutter. Then I tell Alice, "Created a monster, vee haff!"

She says, "Speak for yourself."

Now Gillian cries, "Mr. Allenby says–!"

"Yes, my sweet?" I ask.

"–he's getting left out."

I stroke her cheek, then pat her elephant's ear. "Sorry, we do get carried away. Do you think he'll forgive us?"

After listening to him, she announces, "He wants to know what happens next."

·

6

Hope from the Sea

ON THE FIRST DAY OF the New Year, the islanders gathered on the beach below the castle. William and Alison stood with Avery and their sons among the common folk. Morna and Fiona sat in the royal stall at the base of the cliff. Behind them sat the earl marshall and Lilian. On either side of the stall rose the pavilions of knights from foreign lands. Although they had come to win Fiona's hand in marriage, they admired Lilian's beauty and grace. The Knights of Glandis had remained in Castle Gloom. No one spoke. They were waiting for the sorcerer's curse to appear.

Suddenly, lightning struck. The earth opened, and from its smoking bowels rode a dark warrior. Clad from head to foot in black armour, he carried a black lance and a black shield. The crest on his helmet was a raven, which turned this way and that. His black steed snorted smoke from flared nostrils while it pawed the ground.

"Ooh," Gillian says.

Neil echoes, for Mr. Allenby, "Ooh."

In a voice that made people shiver, the warrior called, "Who dares challenge the Dark Knight?"

The earl marshall rose. "Our first champion," he announced, "is Amadis the Tall." The people cheered, for they knew him to be a noble, young warrior.

He stopped his grey steed in front of Princess Fiona and tilted his lance.

•

82

"The gods be with you," she called.

"Hang on a sec," Neil says. "How did all the foreign knights get to Glandis if the ships keep sinking?"

Alice smiles at me as if asking, "Well?"

"Oh," I say, "the sorcerer was so sure he'd win the crown that, um, the only time it's safe to sail to Glandis is around Christmas and New Year's."

"Alaric never said that," Neil announces.

"Neither did Avery," Gillian adds.

I claim, "I forgot."

Now Alice smiles as if saying, "Nice try."

Sir Amadis took his place opposite the Dark Knight and they lowered their lances. Trumpets sounded, and the warriors charged. "Onward!" the people shouted. "Onward!" Sir Amadis and the Dark Knight met with a fearful clash. When Sir Amadis fell backward, the people groaned. He had been pierced through the heart.

"Oh, no!" Gillian cries.

"Oh, no!" Neil adds.

They turn to Alice and she gasps, "Oh, no!"

Eight more challengers fought the Dark Knight. None could even unseat him. Some, he killed; others, he wounded. Having lost hope, the people began drifting home.

"Are there no more challengers?" the Dark Knight asked. The raven on his helmet eyed the pavilions.

The earl marshall shook his head.

"I'll fight you!" Raedwald cried. He ran forward and fell on one knee before the queen.

Morna looked surprised. "A squire?" she exclaimed. "A mere boy?"

"Nonsense!" the earl marshall said.

"Remember," Lilian told Fiona. "Your mother owes my family

·

a boon."

"Knight the boy, Mother," Fiona pleaded. "Let's call him the Knight of the Red."

Before Morna could speak, William stepped forward. "Lilian," he asked, "how can you send your brother to his death at such an early age?"

"I'm sorry, Father," she replied, "but the time has come to test his prowess. You can't stop him from fighting. Besides, didn't you always wish your sons could become knights?"

Surprise left him mute. He had never told her of his dream.

"Then how did she know?" Neil demands.

"Because," Gillian says, "she's special."

Morna handed her mace to the earl marshall and stepped onto the beach. She drew her sword. While she tapped Raedwald's right shoulder, then his left, she declared, "In the name of all the gods, I dub you Knight of the Red. Be brave, ready and loyal, good Sir Raedwald."

"All right!" Neil exclaims.

"Yay!" Gillian adds.

A white wave appeared on the churning sea. It bore a sword and helmet, a coat of mail, and a red lance and shield. After leaving them on shore, the wave folded back into the water. William ordered Avery to fetch the armour and help Raedwald dress for battle. The earl marshall himself brought a roan stallion. After mounting the horse, Raedwald faced the sea with his back to the cliff. The Dark Knight faced the cliff with his back to the sea. When the trumpets blared, both knights charged. William could hear nothing but the clop of hooves.

Neil clucks his tongue to make a low, clopping sound.

When I pretend to glare at him, Alice chuckles.

.

"What's going on?" Gillian asks.

All Glandis was holding its breath.

"Oh."

The black lance struck the red shield squarely, and Raedwald jolted to the ground. He rose, aching, to his knees.

How the people groaned.

"Do you yield?" the Dark Knight asked. His black steed reared above Raedwald.

"Never!" Raedwald shouted. He grasped the Dark Knight's lance and pulled him to the ground.

Both warriors drew their swords. The Dark Knight fell on Raedwald. Blow after blow rang out while he tried to defend himself. His armour glistened with blood. But while the Dark Knight wasted stroke after stroke, Raedwald fought with skill. Instead of hacking and blocking, he used his strong wrists to thrust and parry. Then he slipped. The Dark Knight dropped his shield. Raising his sword with both hands, he held the point above Raedwald. The Dark Knight laughed in triumph.

"Oh, no!" Gillian gasps.

Neil, mesmerized, is speechless.

Raedwald lunged. His blade pierced the Dark Knight's visor. Black blood gushed from the raven helmet, and the people cheered. The Dark Knight fell dead.

"Yes!" Neil exclaims even as Gillian calls out, "Yay!"

Laughing and crying at the same time, Alison ran toward Raedwald. She stopped when the earth opened. It swallowed the Dark Knight's body and his black horse.

Raedwald walked into the surf. The white wave rolled ashore, lifted him like a child, and carried him out to sea. William stared, dumbfounded. Alison cried, "No!"

Gillian and Neil are suitably moved, but Alice fidgets with the cushion at the small of her back. "If I could interrupt?" she says. "Isn't this a rather violent story? Especially for a little girl's bedtime."

"I'm not a little girl," Gillian insists.

"Life is violent," I say.

"Yeah, Mom," Neil adds.

"Armour glistening with blood!" Alice says. "Blades piercing visors! Oh, Vikram! It's all so ... graphic."

"I'm trying to paint pictures, here," I say. "With words. Graphic, yes. Gratuitous, no."

"It has to be violent, Mom," Neil adds. "Otherwise it wouldn't matter so much when things turn out fine in the end."

"How do you know how things will turn out?" I ask.

"Because," he says. Then, "Don't you?"

"Heck, no," I claim. "I'm making it up as I go along."

He doesn't look convinced.

We're leaving Gillian out again, so I ask her, "What do you think, my sweet?"

She declares, "Mr. Allenby says it's okay as long as Raedwald comes back."

Patting his trunk, I say, "He's a very wise elephant."

"But where did Raedwald go?" she asks.

I try to say, "Back to the sea," but Neil replies, "He's with the Dolphin Liberation Front."

"Oh, good," she says.

I ask Neil, "May I?" Then I look at Alice.

She spreads her hands as if to say, "Who's stopping you?"

That evening, the islanders made merry for the first time in years, but William's household could not join in. He and Alison still grieved over having lost Raedwald. Yet they felt proud of him, especially when Morna commanded them to visit her.

She no longer slouched on her throne. Even her bedraggled knights looked younger and bolder than they had. "Bowman," she said, "a sentry has found six sets of arms washed up on the beach. It's a sign. Hope once came to me while I walked along the shore. Hope has once more come from the sea. Have your sons kneel so that may dub them knights."

William nodded sadly, and they obeyed.

Morna drew her sword. "Only these young men," she told her court, "can free us from the spell."

"Guess she doesn't know about Nigel," Neil says.

"She can't," Gillian tells him. "She's only a queen."

"Wouldn't you like to be a queen?" he asks.

"I'd rather be a princess! Or a lady like Lilian. I'm learning to read, too. And play music." Gillian wiggles her fingers to remind him how she sees the world: not only through Mr. Allenby but also through sound and smell and touch.

Alice is sitting with her hands clasped while she blinks at the floor. She knows I'm watching her, and she gives me a smile that's bravely sad. Or sadly brave. She's anticipating my own feelings—feelings she knows all too well. She has always been the strong one, not I. Even after all these years, it mystifies me—how helpless a father can feel. And yet I try to count our blessings: two, fine children. Still, when I try to continue, I find I have to clear my throat. She pretends not to notice.

On the morning of the second day, the people of Glandis once again gathered on the beach. William and Alison watched with the common folk, but their sons now sat outside a large pavilion. In front of it stood six poles. Each bore a pennon and a matching shield. Avery kept a proud watch over six sets of arms.

When the second curse emerged from the ground, the

·

people fell back with fear. Before them stood a three-eyed ogre with pointed teeth. It crouched until its hands swung below its knees. Then it roared and beat the ground with its fists.

"Ooh," Gillian says.

Once more, Neil echoes, "Ooh."

The sons of William and Alison watched older warriors arm themselves. First came Cid Ahmed Bengeli, the Moorish Knight. After riding as close as he dared, he flung a spear at the ogre. It caught the spear and broke the shaft in two. Before Cid Ahmed could ride back for another spear, the ogre bounded forward and knocked him from his horse. It tore him apart and sucked his flesh from his armour.

"Oh, Vikram!" Alice exclaims.

Neil gives her a look that says, "Don't worry, Mom."

Sickened by the gore, the people watched in horror while the ogre doubled in size. It stood as high as a castle wall. Four knights charged from four different directions. The ogre won with ease. It kicked up a sandstorm, and two of the horses threw their riders. The ogre lifted the other two knights from their saddles. This time, it swallowed the knights whole. While it once again grew, the people became terrified. Now it stood as high as a castle tower.

The earl marshall called out warriors' names. None came forward. At last he called, "Sir Oswald, Knight of the Orange."

Oswald rose onto his long legs and drew his sword. Without taking up his shield, he approached the ogre. It roared and bent to pick him up but he ran between its feet and stabbed its heel. Black blood stained the sand. Howling with fury, the ogre turned to catch him, but it was so huge that it moved with great effort. He ran behind it again. This time, he stabbed the other heel. The ogre turned, but Oswald moved so swiftly that he looked like an

•

orange blur. Round and round the ogre spun until it became too groggy, too dizzy to see. It rubbed its three eyes, then flung its arms wildly. Too tired to take another step, Oswald fell to his knees.

"Uh oh," Gillian tells Mr. Allenby.

Sir Edward, Knight of the Yellow, advanced. Hefting a spear with his oak-strong arm, he stopped out of the ogre's long reach. Then he leaned back and flung the spear. It struck the ogre's middle eye. Screaming with pain, the ogre gnashed its teeth and flailed its arms. Edward tried to help Oswald rise, but the ogre knocked them into the air. They fell in the surf. The ogre toppled, dead, to the ground.

"Yay!" Gillian cries.

Alison ran toward her two, brave sons, but once again the white wave surged forward. It lifted them gently and carried them out to sea. The ogre's body turned into black slime, which oozed into the sand.

While the islanders rejoiced, William tried to comfort Alison. "Don't cry, dear," he said. "We did our duty by raising the three boys. At least we know they're not dead. Besides, we still have four sons with us. You'll see. They won't all leave."

"Oh, good," Gillian says.

Neil can see the chapter has ended on an ironic note, but he doesn't want to disappoint his sister. He nods at me as if to say, "Good one, Dad." Then he does say, for her benefit, "Yup."

Alice rises, claps her hands once, and says, "Right."

Then, for the third time this week, we carry out our nightly ritual. Kisses for Gillian. "Night, night, my sweet." The lamp turned off. The door half closed. The three of us—Alice, Neil and I—settled in the family room while Mr. Allenby leads Gillian to his dreamland.

Not in living colour, she says. Cartoons.

·

7

The Curse of the Third Day

HERE WE ARE AGAIN, for the fourth time this week, gathered in Gillian's room. And—

On the morning of the third day, the people of Glandis gathered on the beach once more. For the first time, Morna's knights rode behind her carriage. They had come to watch, though; they had not come to fight.

Lightning flashed. The sea bubbled and boiled. A serpent emerged from the shoals. Its scales shone a greenish-black. From its hissing mouth darted a forked tongue. Coils slithered behind its head, and last came a tail lashing the water's surface. Once more the sons of William and Alison watched older warriors battle the curse. Five Northmen, armed with axes and bows, pulled their boat into the water. Long ago, William had hated the Northmen for trying to plunder his land, but now even he cheered them on. The serpent attacked. It swallowed one of them whole. The others rowed undaunted; but, before they could reach the serpent, they found themselves attacked from above. Three hygriffs, creatures with eagles' bodies and lions' heads, swooped from the clouds.

"Three what?" Neil asks.

"Hygriffs," I repeat.

"There's no such thing," he says.

"There are now."

•

Flashing their claws, the hygriffs dove at the Northmen. Their leader lost his balance and fell overboard. The serpent slid under the waves. Moments later, it reappeared with his limp body between its fangs. When the other Northmen tried to shoot down the hygriffs, the serpent capsized their boat. The men drowned, and their horned helmets bobbed in the shoals.

The earl marshall called for new challengers but no one armed himself. The sight of a serpent and three fierce hygriffs made the foreign knights quail. Once more he called on the sons of William and Alison.

"Why didn't he do that in the first place?" Gillian asks.

"Because they're the youngest," Neil replies. "Besides, it's a way of building suspense."

"But everybody knows that the foreign knights can't do any good," Gillian says.

Alice smiles at me during this exchange. She's reminding me not to become impatient; to enjoy our children's precocity while it lasts. If I have my way, it will last. They'll never grow into boring adults. "Like us?" Alice asked me once when I mentioned this. "Like I was before we met," I told her. To which she said, "You say the sweetest things."

What a long time ago that was. How hard it is now to imagine life without Gillian or Neil.

"Earth to Dad," he says, and she giggles.

"He's lost in space again," she tells Mr. Allenby.

Now Alice is smiling because I'm looking at her fondly. She arches her eyebrows in a come hither look. After I insist, "Am not," she mouths, "Right."

Sir Godwin, Knight of the Green, strode to the shore. He clutched his bow. On his back hung a quiver of arrows. His large, keen eyes pierced the clouds, and his first arrow felled a hygriff.

·

Screeching with fury, the other two circled above him.

"Hold them off!" someone shouted. Sir Baldwin, Knight of the Blue, ran past his brother. "Serpents must surface to breathe," Baldwin said. "I'll force it underwater for as long as I can." He dashed into the waves and dove out of sight. So did the serpent. Water foamed while it struggled with the barrel-chested boy.

Gillian and Neil, together: "Uh-oh."

Meanwhile, Godwin shot a second hygriff when it swooped. Before he could notch another arrow, the last hygriff scratched out his eyes.

"Oh, Vikram," Alice says.

"Mo-om," Neil says, "it's o-kay."

"Don't worry," Gillian tells Mr. Allenby. "It's not real."

When I ask, "It's not?" she shakes her head. "But you can see everything that's going on? You can almost smell the sea?"

She shakes her head again. Still, to humour me, she adds, "Mr. Allenby hears the waves." Then she sighs. "Poor Godwin."

"No!" William shouted even as Godwin staggered blindly.

"Help him!" Alison cried.

"It's been years since I fought," William said.

With an arrow on his bowstring, Godwin stood alone. He listened carefully. High above him circled the last hygriff. Then it shrieked and swooped for the kill. He leaned back, bent his bow, and shot. The hygriff plunged to earth. When he heard the peoples' cheers, he stumbled toward the sea. He notched a fourth arrow and waded into the surf. A bubble burst the water's surface. The serpent's body rose, belly up, to bob in the swell. Baldwin floated next to the serpent with his arms clasped around its throat. When the people cheered again, Godwin threw down his bow and quiver. Once again the white wave rolled ashore. It

.

lifted the two brothers and carried them out to sea.

While the serpent sank, the earth opened to swallow the hygriffs. The people went mad with joy.

William picked up Godwin's weapons and stared at them. "I hoped at least you would stay," he muttered. He looked at what remained of his family and said, "Godwin could have helped me fish and hunt, as he did in the old days."

"No, Father," Lilian said. She had stepped down from the royal stall. "Godwin wasn't born to be a fisherman. My brothers came with the tide, and like the tide they must leave."

"What will happen next?" Alison asked. "Tell us."

"I can't," Lilian said. She returned to her place behind Fiona.

"Princess of Glandis," Gillian reminds Mr. Allenby.

William placed an arm about Alison's shoulder. He realized he had never understood his daughter. Just as Godwin had not been born to become a fisherman, so Lilian had not been born to marry and keep house. "It's clear to me now," he told Alison. "Lilian has always known more than she has told us."

"Boy," Neil says, "is he slow or what?" Then, "Is that it?"

"It's a short chapter," I say.

Gillian, nodding, adds, "Short and sweet."

8

Princess of Glandis

ON THE MORNING OF THE fourth day, a great commotion awoke
Morna. Fiona's ladies-in-waiting burst into the queen's chamber.
Except for Lilian, they were all in tears.

"She's gone!" a lady said. "But we didn't hear her leave!"

"Fiona has vanished!" another cried.

I wait for Neil and Gillian to say, "Oops," but they don't.

"Guards," Morna called, "search every inch of the castle!" An
hour later, she slouched on her throne once more. The guards
had found no trace of Fiona. "She's been stolen away by the
sorcerer," Morna groaned. She blinked back tears.

"Your Majesty," the earl marshall said, "if you appear like this
in front of your subjects, they'll lose the faith they've regained in
you."

Morna wiped the tears from her haggard face. "For Fiona's
sake, I brought this terrible spell on Glandis. Is there any reason
to fight now that she's gone?"

The earl marshall helped her rise. "Yes," he said, "for your
people."

Soon, while Morna took her place in the royal stall, her
subjects cheered. Few of them noticed the empty place in front
of Lilian, where Fiona should have been. Down the cliff rolled a

black cloud trailing fog. It stopped in the middle of the beach. When the fog lifted, the people gasped. Morna cried out. Fiona stood tied to a stake within a ring of boulders. Fires burned in a wide circle on the sand. They spread slowly inward.

Again, I wait, this time for Neil and Gillian to cry, "Oh, no!" But, once again, they remain silent.

Morna leapt to her feet. "Save the princess!" she cried. "I'll give anything to the man who rescues her!"

At this, all the remaining knights from foreign lands leapt into their saddles. William's remaining sons did not move. Nor did the Knights of Glandis.

"Here's our chance," Avery told William. "We could win our fortune!"

William crossed his arms and stood firm. "It's too late to join the battle of younger men."

Neil says, "Methinks yon Bowman protests too much."

I pretend to scowl, and Alice laughs. "Neil's showing off again," she tells Gillian.

"Typical," Gillian says. She tells Mr. Allenby, "Just you watch. It'll get him in trouble again."

"Again?" Alice asks.

"Neil said once that Ms. Mcaulay said—"

Neil interrupts with, "Not now, Gilly! The princess is in a pickle."

When she asks, as she did earlier in the week, "What kind of pickle?" he laughs and says, "Good one."

Two dozen steeds leapt the flames and galloped toward the boulders. The first knight to reach them brandished his sword. Yet, even as he guided his horse between two rocks, they rumbled, then rolled together to crush him. And crush his horse. Other knights dismounted and tried to slip between the boulders.

·

Within minutes, these knights, too, had fallen.

"Help me!" Fiona cried. Then her eyes opened wide and she shook her head. "No, go back! Save yourselves!"

The fires had burned closer. None of the remaining horses could jump the wide circle of flames, and so the last of the foreign knights burned to death.

Eyeing me with her chin tucked, Alice shakes her head.

"Look at it this way," Neil tells her. "Fiona's stopped being selfish."

"Leona's not selfish," Gillian says.

"Fiona," Neil repeats. "The one whose name means 'the white one.'"

"We still like Lilian better," Gillian tells Mr. Allenby.

"If you don't mind me saying so," I tell the room at large, "we're slowing down the pacing."

"Well then," Alice declares, "as Mr. Allenby would say, 'We're all ears.'"

Giggling, Gillian pokes her elephant. "That's telling them."

Neither Sir Ivor nor Sir Wystan waited for the earl marshall to call on them. They dashed forward. Wystan climbed onto Ivor's back. With a run and a jump, the boy with the hefty thighs leapt easily over the flames. But when he landed, Ivor slipped on blood and struck his head on charred armour. Wystan tumbled between two boulders. They rolled together.

The circle of fire burned so high that William could barely see what went on. At last, through the shimmering haze, he saw the boulders part. Wystan had braced his feet against one boulder and his back against another. His muscular belly strained so hard, links of mail flew from his violet armour. With a mighty yell, he straightened his legs. The boulders shattered. He called to his brother in a voice so weak, it barely carried.

Ivor rose groggily. He stumbled through the passage Wystan

•

had made, then cut Fiona's bonds. She cried with relief while he took her onto his back and tied her wrists in front of him. He took a short run and leapt high, so high that both of them might just as well have flown. Then they descended to land out of danger. Ivor released Fiona, who collapsed into Morna's arms. Morna brushed soot from Fiona's golden hair. Both of them raised their eyes in time to see Ivor jump back over the flames. Wystan was still trapped.

An enormous white wave gathered force on the dark sea.

"There's that wave again," Neil says.

People ran for cover while the wave surged ashore, but it did not touch them. It swept over the beach and put out the fire with a long hiss. When it folded back into the sea, it carried away the bodies of horses and men, the boulders and stake, and the last two sons of William and Alison.

"Aw," Gillian says.

"Don't worry," Neil tells her. "They'll be back."

"Now, now," Alice tells him, "we don't want to steal your father's thunder."

"We sure don't," I say.

The people celebrated all night. They danced and laughed and listened to minstrels sing ballads about the seven strange boys. Everyone thought they would return to defeat the final curse.

"What did I tell you?" Neil asks.

He grins when Gillian declares, "Everyone thought they would return."'

Morna held court in the castle, and William and Alison stood before the throne. William bore Godwin's bow and quiver. Avery stood with the Knights of Glandis, for he still ached to fight. "You had seven sons," Morna told William, "who vanquished the first four curses. Even if the fifth remains undefeated in my lifetime, I'll die content. Well, perhaps not. But how can I show you my gratitude?"

William looked at Alison before replying. "Your Majesty," he said, "a man needs only two things to be happy: loved ones and land. I have a wife and daughter but no home to call my own. Ever since we arrived, we've lived under other people's roofs. Land is all I want."

"That's easier asked for than given," Morna said. "Glandis is an island. All of its land was long ago divided among my subjects."

"Then give me the shore," William said. "I'm a fisherman by trade."

The earl marshall laughed so hard, his tarnished chain of office clinked. "Have you seen our coast?" he asked. "Monsters breed offshore, not fish."

"Good one," Neil says.

Morna told the earl marshall, "True. At the same time, much good has come to us from the sea." She commanded William, "Kneel," and he obeyed. He placed his hands between hers. Then she declared, "I hereby grant you, William Bowman, the use of the entire coast of Glandis. You can't own it, since all the land in our kingdom belongs to the crown, but perhaps one day you'll be able to fish and hunt in safety."

William knew what he was expected to say. He had said it once to Gerald, long ago: "I vow to serve you as long as I live. Your friends will be my friends. Your enemies will be my enemies." William rose while the Knights of Glandis cheered.

"We need a fitting token of our bond," Morna said. "All my gloves long ago rotted, so I can't give you one." After looking about, she gestured to the earl marshall, who bent so that she could whisper to him. He left the room and returned with a battle axe, one made by Baldwin and Edward. "I'd rather give you a more peaceful token of our bond," she said, "but these are still troubled times. Take heart in knowing who fashioned this axe."

"Um, Dad," Neil says. "Shouldn't that be 'who made this axe'?"

"Why?" I ask.

Gillian turns from Mr. Allenby to look in Neil's direction.

He says, "You said once that shorter words are stronger than longer ones. Longer words can sound ..."

"Archaic," Alice finishes for him.

I can't help laughing. He looks so much like her when she, too, is preparing an argument. It's clear he's not done yet. "The way you told it once," he says, "shorter words tend to be Anglo-Saxon. Longer words tend to be ... Latinate."

Gillian yawns.

"So," he asks, "what kind of word is fashion?"

"Probably Anglo-French," I say. "Fachon. But it would've come from the Old French façon, and that would've come from the Latin factio, which means—"

Alice interrupts to ask, "And what kind of word is make?"

"Old English," I say.

Alice tells Neil, "I think your father tends to use longer words in this story because they sound fairy tale-ish."

"What kind of word is that?" I ask.

"Thing is," he tells me, "this is supposed to be an Anglo-type of story, right? I mean Glandis, like in England. So shouldn't all the words be Anglo-Saxon?"

Alice laughs and laughs. She can't help it, just as I can't help the way I probably look. The word is flabbergasted.

•

"Well then," Neil says. He ends his argument with a line Alice would love to deliver in court: "I rest my case."

She applauds.

"Ahem!" Gillian declares. "Ahem?"

"Sorry, my sweet," I say. "This is a side of your brother I never knew existed."

"It's all those cryptic crosswords," Gillian tells Mr. Allenby. She listens as though he's telling her something. "Morna gave William an axe," she says, "that Baldwin and Edward made."

"Yes!" Neil exclaims.

William wrapped his fingers about the solid, wooden handle. The axe made his right arm feel strong. "I don't plan to use it," he said, "for I fought only in my youth. I bear Godwin's arms as a token of my sorrow. Still, I thank Your Majesty." He gestured for Avery to step forward. "Since there are no more knights in my household," William declared, "your days as my servant are ended. You may call yourself Shipman once more."

Avery beamed. Then he shrugged. "You need land to be happy. I need a ship. Until I can steer one away from here, I'll serve you as a freeman because you are just."

Removing the bow and quiver from his shoulder, William said, "Take these, then, as a token of our new bond."

Avery did so and bowed.

Alison clapped while the earl marshall cried, "Hurray for the Bowman and his vassal!"

Only Lilian remained silent. She could not feel as happy as everyone else because she remembered what they had forgotten. "One more curse," she thought. "How can they guess it will be the most dreadful of all?"

For the second time this evening, Neil asks, "Is that it?"

•

100

"Another short chapter," I say.

"Short and sweet," Gillian repeats. Then, plaintively, "But story time's supposed to last half an hour! That's the rule."

"Didn't this one?" I ask.

"That was more like fifteen minutes! I can tell."

Glancing at his watch, Neil says, "Sixteen and a half."

"Oh dear," I tell Alice.

"Don't look at me," she says.

"That's the rule," Gillian reminds Mr. Allenby. "No TV before bedtime, and Mommy reads to us for half an hour. Or Neil does."

"Or Dad tells a story," Neil says.

"So you have to tell us what happens in the end," Gillian insists.

"How do you know we're coming to the end?" I ask.

"I can tell," she says.

"You're right, my sweet. We are. Problem is, I'm not sure what happens next. I'll figure it out tomorrow and tell you tomorrow night."

"You mean you don't know?" Neil asks.

I wag my head: maybe yes, maybe no.

As always, Alice saves the day. Rising, she tells Gillian, "Daddy's had his fifteen minutes. Now I get mine. What book has Neil been reading you?"

I sigh my thanks to her. Even as I bend to kiss Gillian good night, she says, "It's on the chest of drawers. Anne of Green Gables. We just started."

Surprised at the choice, I look at Neil and ask, "Really?"

He looks abashed, as though a boy shouldn't be interested by Anne or Marilla. "It's a very funny book," he insists. "The way Anne goes on and on. Then there's her recital of The Lady of Shalott, leaky boat and all."

"He keeps laughing," Gillian adds, "and losing his place."

"But I'm sure Mr. Allenby helps him find it again," Alice says. She *turns with the book in her hand.*

"Mr. Allenby's an elephant," *Gillian declares.* *"He's not a bookmark."*

I say, "Night, night," and rise from her bed.

Alice takes my place.

Neil and I, in the doorway now, say, "Night, Mr. Allenby."

On our way to the family room, I put my hand on Neil's shoulder. "You know," I say, "when I was in grade five, our teacher used to read to us. Wind in the Willows. Beautiful Joe. *Our school had a great little library, practically a broom closet. There were these classic anthologies like* Chum's *and* Boys' Own Annual—"

"Anglo-type," he says.

I nod again. "And somewhere in there I found a copy of Anne of Green Gables." *We walk down the few steps to the family room.* "So, one day, when Miss Black asked us what book we'd like next, I piped up, 'Anne of Green Gables'!" *I settle in my favourite chair and place the biography of Einstein in my lap.*

Neil sits on the love seat and places Treasure Island *in his lap.* "Then what happened?" he asks.

"The other boys groaned. Well, a few did, but the rest took it up. You know how boys are."

"I sure do," he says.

"And these weren't even awful boys. Well, most of them weren't. But back to the present. What're you planning to read Gillian next?"

"Heidi," *he announces, not at all abashed.*

"Good choice," I say.

Then we open our books and read until we hear Alice say, "Night, night." We look up while she comes down those few steps to join us. She smiles. She knows that this looking up from a book is our way of rising when a woman enters the room.

"You're right," she tells Neil. "It is a very funny book." She sits in her

•

favourite chair and picks up her biography of Marie Curie. Alice doesn't open it at once. She looks at Gillian's piano. As usual, Gillian practised for an hour today, after Neil walked her home from her school. Next spring, she'll compete in our local music festival. She'll win her category again— if only because she doesn't play to win. She plays for herself. And for us. I wonder what might happen if she doesn't win, though I wouldn't dare ask Alice about this. It annoys her that I expect so much from our children but I can't help myself. This was how my sisters and I were raised. Is it any surprise that the older one has become the first female department head at her hospital? Or that the younger one is a managing partner of her IT firm? It puzzles both of them that I gave up a promising career in the civil service to stay home and write. Can I help it if I'm not as competitive as they are?

When Alice says, "We really are very lucky," I realize I've been frowning at the piano. She says this every so often and I agree with her, but I can never bring myself to say these words aloud. Maybe I'm superstitious. No maybe—I know I am. This is why I have to remind myself to praise our children when praise is due. Why I have to remind myself that the evil eye watches somewhere else, far away, in a country I haven't seen these forty years. It still amazes me: the older I get, the less I know about India and yet the more Indian I feel. I can just hear my parents chuckling, up there in heaven, while they wait to be reborn. I can just see them, too: my father not knowing what to do with all this time on his hands; my mother gossiping with her friends over endless games of whist.

Finally, I nod to Alice. Yes, we really are very lucky.

Neil has been waiting for the moment to pass. Only now does he sit up to ask, "Say, Dad. Where did you get the idea for this story? What's it called, by the way?"

"'The Rainbow Knights,'" *I reply.*

Both he and his mother nod as if saying, "Of course."

.

"Where did I get the idea?" I close my book. "Do you want the long version or the short version?"

"The short version," Alice says.

Neil grins.

"In that library in my school," I say, "there was a book called The Five Chinese Brothers—"

"I remember that one," Alice says, "but wasn't it called The Seven Chinese Brothers?"

"Could be there are different versions floating around. No, I know there are. I checked at the public library last week—when I got the idea for 'The Rainbow Knights'—because something about William and Alison's boys seemed familiar. Turns out, the version I remember—with the five brothers—is from the thirties. It was written and illustrated by two Americans, I think. The funny thing is, I remembered the illustrations as being in full colour, but they're really in yellow and black—"

"I think we're getting the long version," Alice tells Neil.

He surprises us by musing, "Yellow for the yellow peril?"

Stunned, Alice covers her mouth.

"I never thought of that," I say. "Point is, neither the writer or the illustrator had Chinese names."

"Nor the illustrator," Neil says.

"Thanks," I tell him. "But the library also has a version with six brothers—"

"Oh, brother," Neil says.

"—and this version's written and illustrated by the same person. You'll be glad to know that his name is Chinese. The illustrations are scissor cuts by the author. Printed in red and black."

"You still haven't answered my question," he says.

"Which was?"

"Having trouble with our short-term memory, are we?" He repeats,

•

slowly, "Where did you get the idea for The Rainbow Knights'?"

"Didn't I just say?"

"Not unless I dozed off somewhere," Alice replies.

"Oh, sorry. From trying to read Don Quixote—last week—and from remembering the Chinese brothers. Do you know the story?" I ask Neil.

He shakes his head.

"Each brother has something odd about him. Depending on which version you read, one boy has iron bones, another one loves heat, and so on. Anyway, one of them gets into trouble and he's condemned to death. But the day he's supposed to be beheaded, the brother with the iron bones takes his place. The day he's supposed to be burned alive, the one who loves heat takes his place. And so on, till the first brother is finally pardoned. In between, they go home to say good-bye to their mother—in some versions. Their father, in others."

"I've missed something," Neil tells Alice.

"Oh, I forgot!" I say. "All the brothers look alike."

"Minor detail," Alice tells Neil.

"So, last week, when I thought of making up a story about rainbows and knights, I remembered the one about the Chinese brothers—or I misremembered it, the coloured illustrations—and that's why each of the boys Alaric sends William and Alison has something wrong with him."

"Something special about him," Neil says.

"Right. But this is a modern-day fairy tale, so I didn't want a man to save the day. I didn't want the heroine to be the princess, all helpless and—"

"Save me, save me!" Neil says in a high-pitched voice.

"—hapless. That's why all the twists."

"You mean there are more?" he asks.

Smiling, I open my book and Alice says, "Vikram, don't smirk." I try

·

to say, "I don't smirk," even as she tells Neil, "Don't forget Lilian."

"Why, Mumsy!" he exclaims, as though he's quoting from Chum's or The Boys' Own Annual. "I would never forget Gillian-Lilian."

To which Alice says, "Prithee, curb thy florid tongue."

But even as he stretches out again, he asks, "Say, Dad, did you draw a map of Glandis?"

Now, what?

"You know I can't draw," I say.

"RLS drew a map of Treasure Island for his stepson."

Alice asks, "RLS?"

"Robert Louis Stevenson. That's what people called him. I looked him up at the library after—" He raises and lowers his book. "—I started this. The stepson's name was Lloyd Osbourne. The way I read it, he got sick and so, every day, RLS wrote a new chapter of Treasure Island for him. I told Mrs. Macaulay—" She's his English teacher but, no, her first name isn't Earl. "—and she said, instead of writing a book report, why don't I write an essay about how Treasure Island came to be written?"

"You have such good teachers," Alice says.

I ask him, "Are you telling me that, as soon as this book arrived, you sat down and read a whole bio of ... RLS?"

He shrugs. "Didn't take long. I found it in the children's section. That's what you do, right, when you retell those Indian legends? You said you start with the comic book, then you read the children's book, then you work your way up to the adult—"

I laugh with delight while Alice grins at me. Shaking my head, I exclaim, "So much for trade secrets!"

"Do I detect another story writer in the family?" Alice asks.

"Heck, no," Neil says. "I'm going to be a lawyer. Just like you."

"That's very sweet," she says. She does look touched.

"Sweet, nothing," he says. "RLS died young on an island in the

·

South Pacific. When I die, I'm going to be a supreme court justice. Gilly's the artist in the family."

Alice looks at me and I look at her, but neither of us is prepared for what comes next.

"Let's face it," Neil announces. "It's like Mom said about Auntie Nirmala. They'll never appoint an Indian to the bench here, but maybe they'll appoint a half-Indian. Comme moi, *par example. I can always write fiction after I retire."*

Shaking her head in wonder, Alice looks to me to say something, so I do: "That's, um, rather farsighted of you, son. Maybe after I retire from writing fiction, I'll join the supreme court."

"Good one, Dad," he says.

"I don't think it was original," Alice tells him. "Your father seems to have an ear for precedents."

"Presidents?" I ask.

Chuckling, Neil returns to his book.

Opening her own book at last, Alice looks at me as if to say, "Nice try."

I don't open my own book yet. I'm too wrapped up in imagining what I'll say when I'm old and grey and showing family photos to strangers in the park. "This is our son, Neil, the supreme court justice. And this is our daughter, Gillian, the concert pianist. Oh, and here are our grandchildren. The boy's named Vik, after me. And the girl's named Alice, of course . . ."

·

9

The Return of the Sun

ON THE MORNING OF THE fifth day, the islanders woke full of hope. Soon, though, they despaired. It had rained all night. Now a fog rolled in from the sea. Alison stood under a canopy reserved for gentlewomen. William leaned on his battle axe nearby. Proudly bearing the bow and quiver, Avery stood behind him.

Gillian pokes Mr. Allenby and whispers, "That's you."

Lightning flashed. Thunder boomed. A hot wind cleared the beach of fog to reveal a tall man dressed in black. His face looked as pale as ice; yet his eyes glowed like a beast's. His fingernails were so long, his hands looked like claws. At his feet lay two black lizards with fiery eyes. Some of the islanders inched forward to see better but they jumped back when he scowled.

"People of Glandis," he said, "you have been lucky! You have defeated the first four curses. Now look upon the fifth and tremble! It is I, the sorcerer once loved by your queen. By spurning me, she condemned you to eighteen years of suffering. I am the King of Darkness, Emperor of the Night. Who will dare challenge me?"

"Roy G. Biv," Neil says.

"Shh," Gillian warns.

Alice nods at him.

•

William looked about and shook his head with dismay. All the foreign knights were dead. His seven sons were gone. Only the Knights of Glandis remained. Clad in rusty armour, each seated beside his scraggly horse, they made a pitiful sight. When none of them came forward, the sorcerer stamped his foot.

The lizards rose to hiss while he growled, "What! Is there not one courageous being on this island? I took your measure well. You are all cowards."

"Not all," a girl cried. "I challenge you."

"We're up," Gillian tells Mr. Allenby.

Neil grins as if to say, "I should've known."

Everyone stared in amazement when Lilian stepped down from the royal stall. She wore a hooded, white cape over a white gown. When she threw back her hood, the people gasped. They had never seen a lovelier maiden.

Laughing, the sorcerer flung his cape clear of his pale arms. "You?" he asked. "A puny girl? Hah!"

"Come back," Alison called.

Lilian refused to stop.

Laughing shrilly, the sorcerer snapped his fingers. Thunderbolts appeared above his head. When he pointed at her, the thunderbolts attacked.

Lilian stopped at last. She raised her hands though she bore no weapon. Water bubbled from the sand and rose to form a blue-green wall around her. The thunderbolts battered at this wall and the water turned to steam. The sorcerer cast more thunderbolts. She held them off. Then her power waned and they flashed in her eyes. When she covered her face, the wall of water fell. "Father," she cried, "help me!" The thunderbolts exploded. They engulfed her in a ball of fire.

·

"Uh-oh," Gillian says.

Neil is speechless.

Alice eyes me as if saying, "You be careful."

All Glandis cried out. Alison screamed; Morna clutched her fur collar; the knights hung their heads in shame.

William choked with anger. At last he realized what he had to do. He raised his axe. "People of Glandis," he said, "you all know me. I came here with my family because this kingdom promised us refuge from evil. But we found something worse than evil on this island. We found fear. Our sons defeated the first four curses. Our daughter challenged the fifth when even I didn't dare. How much longer will you wait for a champion? It's time to fight for yourselves!"

Even as he spoke, the fireball rose from the beach.

Gillian whispers to Mr. Allenby, "We're flying!"

"I'm invincible," the sorcerer screamed. "One flick of my finger can turn you to stone."

"Do it," William shouted. "I know your kind. You've never turned a man to stone. Your weapon is nothing more than fear." He grasped his axe with both hands. "I thought it's better to live in peace than die in battle. How wrong I was. I would rather die free than live like a slave!"

The fireball rose even higher. Regaining their courage, the Knights of Glandis mounted their horses and drew their swords.

The sorcerer snarled at William, "You lead these scarecrows to their doom. Cower, fool, while I cast my final spell!" He crouched and twirled. His cape flapped in the wind. His voice grew even more shrill while he rose to his full height and chanted these words:

I, King of Darkness, Emperor of the Night

Summon all my forces into sight.
Demons of fire, damp earth, cold air
Spring, creep, slither, dive from your lair.
Rage, blinding snow! Pelt, crippling hail!
Prove to these mortals I cannot fail.
He pointed a claw-like hand at William.

"Deny my power and draw your last breath, While I turn this Dark Isle to the Island of Death!"

Neil gasps.

"Mommy," Gillian calls. "Daddy's a poet and he doesn't know it. But his feet do. They're …"

"Longfellows," Alice finishes.

Neil says, "Not now, Gilly." He rarely pleads with her like this. Only four nights ago, he was "just passing by."

Fiery demons crawled from the earth. Slimy demons oozed from the cliff. Though they stood no taller than dwarves, they were more terrifying than giants. Prancing on hoofed feet, they gnashed their fangs and spat brimstone. Demons of the air swooped from the clouds. The people shivered with fear until snow and hail made them shiver with cold. While they left the beach, the fireball slowly fell.

Gillian: "Uh-oh."

The sorcerer cackled in triumph. "Where is your courage now?" he asked. His lizards growled, then lay at his feet.

William raised his voice above the shriek of demons and the howl of winds. "People of Glandis, look!" He chanted the riddle carved on the cliff:

To find the sun who hides from sight,
Take heart, and with your shadows fight,
For Glandis can never be truly free

Till a rainbow curves from sky to sea.

"These creatures are your shadows. They're nothing more than your own fears, and see how small they are!"

At this, one of the flying demons swooped at William from behind. The earl marshall drew his sword, pushed William aside, and struck the creature down.

The Knights of Glandis cheered.

"See?" William asked. "Faith will aid a man whose arm is weak but whose courage returns. Evil can feed only on fear. For Glandis!" He beheaded a demon of fire.

The earl marshall beheaded yet another. "For freedom!" he cried.

The fireball rose higher than ever. Morna's knights lowered their lances. They shouted, "For Glandis! For freedom!" and they charged.

Gillian: "Yay!"

Neil: "Hoo-ray!"

Alice applauds.

A flying demon tried to snatch at Fiona. Morna fought it off with her mace. Avery notched an arrow and shot the demon. Wielding lance and blade, Morna's knights cut down their foe.

Colours swirled in the fireball and tried to break free.

The sorcerer stood in the midst of the beach and urged his demon soldiers onward. Lightning blared like trumpets; thunder boomed like drums. Blood and snow turned the sand to red mud.

William paused wearily. For every demon he killed, two more seemed to take its place. Black blood coated his axe. After wiping the blade, he looked up. The next moment, his voice rang clearly through the din: "The rainbow!"

The battle stopped.

•

The fireball had sent out seven rays, each a different colour: red, orange, yellow, green, blue, indigo, and violet. They pointed at the sea.

"Roy G. Biv!" Gillian exclaims.

Neil nods silently.

"That's right," Alice tells Gillian.

Morna flourished her mace above her head. "There's the symbol of our freedom!" she shouted. "Who will follow me now?"

"I will!" a man yelled. Others added, "So will I!"

By dozens, then by hundreds, the people of Glandis swarmed onto the battlefield. Men brandished knives and clubs, mallets and scythes. Women fought with broken lances, dented shields. Children flung rocks. When the last person in Glandis joined the fray, the rainbow struck the sea. The fog lifted. The churning water stilled. Smooth as a mirror now, the sea reflected the rainbow. Then, eight dolphins appeared. They pulled a giant scallop shell. An old man held their reins. Beside him stood a young knight. The wind ruffled his golden hair. His mail flashed every colour of the rainbow and his tunic gleamed pearl white.

"William," Alison shouted, "it's Alaric and, yes, it's our Nigel!"

"Neil," Gillian exclaims, "you're back!"

He gives a drawn-out, "Wo-ow!"

William stopped fighting only long enough to look. "Fight on!" he told the people around him. "Earl Marshall, follow me!"

The giant shell bobbed in the surf. Nigel stepped ashore. He looked eager to join the battle; yet, like Lilian, he bore no weapon. Alaric pointed at the fireball. A silver blade dropped from its midst. Nigel raised an arm with his hand open. Blinded by the flashing sword, demons fled its path. His hand closed on the silver hilt. Alaric raised a conch shell to his lips and blew a single, piercing note.

How the people shivered: with courage, with pride.

Step by step, Nigel fought his way from the shore toward the sorcerer. Slash by slash, William also cleared a path toward the middle of the beach. The earl marshall protected William while Avery shot down demons that swooped at them. Finally, only the lizards stood between William and his goal.

"Destroy him!" the sorcerer shrieked.

The lizards lunged. One knocked the axe from William's grasp. The other sent him sprawling in the mud and bared its fangs. He squeezed his eyes shut. Then, hearing the sorcerer laugh in triumph, William opened his eyes. A silver blade flashed. With a single, mighty blow, Nigel split the sorcerer in two.

Gillian and Neil are open-mouthed.

Alice shakes her head.

The lizards vanished. A pillar of flame shot skyward. The demons of the air flew into the flames. Craters opened to swallow the demons of fire and earth. Once the flames died down, the snow and hail stopped. The clouds parted. A sunbeam bathed Nigel in golden light. He helped William rise. Not knowing what to say, William stared at his long-lost son.

Crying for joy, Alison ran through the crowd, which parted for her. Nigel smiled and opened his arms. "Yes, Mother," he said, "I've come back." She threw herself into his arms. He hugged her while she kissed his blood-stained cheeks, his brow.

Neil blinks at the floor.

Alice wipes at her eyes.

I pretend not to notice.

Alaric stepped ashore. He gestured for Nigel to follow him.

When they stopped in front of the royal stall, only Nigel bowed to the queen.

"Pray," she asked, "who are you?"

"I am Alaric," the old man said, "the Lord of the Deep. This is Sir Nigel, the true son of William Bowman and Alison Fair. To train him for knighthood, I took him from his parents and gave them Lilian and her brothers to raise. It is true that clouds hid the sun in the sky, but Nigel was the son your people had to find by fighting their shadows. Your Majesty ordered the wrong word carved on the cliff."

Gillian laughs and laughs. "We got that! S-o-n."

Neil whispers, "Yup."

Morna laughed heartily at her mistake. "Do we call you the Knight of the Deep?" she asked Nigel.

"No, Your Majesty," he replied. "You may call me the Knight of the Rainbow, for in me are the strength of my brothers and the spirit of my sister."

"I have a new title for you," she said. "Come forward." After Nigel took his place beside her, she gave him Fiona's hand. "Be a good husband to my daughter, Prince Nigel of Glandis."

Morna's knights pointed their swords at him. "Hail, Prince of Glandis!"

"Neil's going to marry Leona?" Gillian exclaims.

"Thanks a lot, Dad," he says.

Laughing, William placed an arm around Alison's shoulder. His dream had more than come true. Not only had his son become a knight, but now he was also a prince.

Morna gestured for William and Alison to step forward. "Well, Bowman," the queen said, "how can I reward you now?"

"You already gave me the shore," he said. "What I did today, I did out of love for my new home. Not for any reward. However, I would be even more grateful if you gave Avery a ship."

"So be it." She told Avery, "The first ship built in Glandis will be yours."

Avery beamed at William.

"As for my people," she said, "I can give you no more than you've earned for yourselves. Weep for the dead, then rejoice for the living. We are free at last!"

All Glandis cheered. Drummers pounded on their drums; trumpeters blew their horns; people joined hands to dance; minstrels broke into song.

Fiona asked Alaric, "What about the boys I knighted?"

"And Lilian?" Alison said.

Alaric pointed at the sky. The fireball had vanished but the rainbow still shimmered in the sun.

To this day, the people of Glandis leave their houses after every storm. They watch the clouds part. They watch their rainbow appear. It is unlike any rainbow you have ever seen for it curves up from the island, past the sun, then down toward the sea. The bands of colour are the trails left by the seven boys. Above them arcs an eighth band, a pure white band, which marks the path Lilian takes while she leads the Rainbow Knights.

The End

Gillian: —

Neil: —

Alice: —

Mr. Allenby: —

•

116

I would have prefered applause but the silence in the room is an even greater reward. I, of all people, feel humbled. And looking down at Gillian—at her face glowing in the light from her lamp—I can't help myself. I have to wipe at my eyes. If only stories could solve the problems of the real world. Then I look at Alice and read the answer in her blue, sapphire eyes. "They can," she's telling me, "for a while. Then we'll need another story. And another. Besides," I imagine her saying, "Our life isn't all that bad, is it?" No, it's not.

At last Neil clears his throat. "Um," he says, "good one, Dad."

Gillian lets go of Mr. Allenby and raises her arms. I bend so she can clasp me about the neck. "Thank you, Daddy," she says.

"You're welcome, my sweet." I stroke her dark hair. We stay like this for the longest time until we hear her mother rising from the floor.

"Right," Alice says.

I kiss Gillian, who lets me go reluctantly. I rise and move to the doorway.

She tells her mother, "It hasn't been half an hour yet."

Neil glances at his watch. He frowns sheepishly at me as if to say, "I lost track."

I smile at him as if to say, "It doesn't matter."

Alice tells Gillian, "I can read you more of Anne.*"*

"Want some music?" Gillian asks.

"I can take a hint," Alice says.

This time Neil and I wait in the hallway while Gillian, clutching Mr. Allenby, leads Alice down the stairs. Then Neil and I follow. Gillian listens to us taking our usual places in the family room. Then she plays the first movement of the Moonlight. *What a large piece for such small hands, and yet she has learned where and how to change the fingering. She can easily sustain the octaves of the left hand, but on the second page and the fourth, when the right hand must span nine notes, she plays the lowest note of the ninth with her left hand even as her right plays continual triplets.*

Beethoven dated his sonata December 1801. Only a few years before this, he contracted the illness that may have led, eventually, to his deafness. I wonder if he knew.

I wonder if he knew where and when and who would play this Sonata in the Style of a Fantasy. He didn't coin its nickname of Moonlight. That was someone else, a critic who attended the premiere and, for whatever reason, loved the moonlight on Lake Lucerne. Maybe he was Swiss. I don't know. But here we are—Alice and I—two centuries later in another world, facing the end of one millennium and the beginning of the next, neither of us knowing what the future holds for our children—our two, fine children—and I look at their mother, who listens with her eyes closed, and I look at our son, who smiles with so much sadness, so much love, and they see what I see, I'm sure of it. Gillian dancing in the moonlight. Gillian twirling away, then returning, always returning although, one day, we will have to let her go.

And, finally, I see what Alice sees; what Neil must see, as well. Gillian doesn't need to be babied. She doesn't want to be babied. She will do just fine. Perhaps she won't become a concert pianist, but what does it matter? She and Neil already have far more than I ever had as a child: two parents under one roof, safety, love. Neil has his wit, even if it does get him into trouble at times. Gillian has her music. She doesn't even need us to read to her—her fingers move as surely across a page of Braille as they do across a keyboard—but we enjoy reading to her, and she enjoys listening. Perhaps it's her way of assuring us that, although she may not need us the way I would like her to need us—to need me—she wants us to do these simple things for her so that we won't feel helpless. So I won't feel helpless. It amazes me, though it shouldn't, not after all these years:

how much wisdom—how much strength—our children bring with them into our world. Alice knows this, and I see by her smile that she's happy for me, happy that I've learned—at long last—what she and Gillian have known all along.

What is the sound of one hand clapping?

It is the sound of moonlight da dancing on the waves.

SUSHILA IS AT HOME

1

The Garden of L

SEATED ON THE LIVING ROOM floor of her posh Calgary home, Sushila unwraps a packet of cigarettes. She places the crinkling cellophane in a wastebasket and drops the packet in her lap. She has brought the basket in here for the litter she will create. She is fanatical about cleanliness, even for a Brahmin. A lighter and a cut-glass ashtray sit on the floor. On the coffee table in front of her are an address book, a felt pen, scissors, tape, a roll of craft paper and, still in its rectangular box, a Fisher-Price Deluxe Discovery Quilt/ *Tapis champêtre.*

When she says, "Good, good," only God hears—Lord Vishnu himself. He can always find time for her. He sits on a nearby sofa with two of his arms spread along its back, the other two at his sides. He admires his reflection in the glassed-in fireplace. She does not look directly at him because she does not want to seem demanding. And so she begins.

The quilt is for the first child, born last week in Vancouver, of Sushila's favourite niece. Padma is not really a niece because Sushila is an only child. But in this vastly extended family, as in many others, one's cousins are one's sisters and brothers. Their children become the children Sushila never had. She likes to think of herself as everyone's favourite aunt and she is, perhaps because she rarely gives advice. "I never interfere," she announces.

·

Vishnu nods reassuringly.

Refusing to interfere is out of character for an Indian aunt, but it is something Sushila learned a decade ago, at fifty, soon after her mother died. Soon after Sushila inherited what she considers her ill fitting mantle of a matriarch. She learned that the best way to earn affection is not to demand it. And the best way to influence family affairs is not to try. This is something Padma's mother still has not learned.

Some years back, while Sushila had been visiting them, Padma had announced, "I don't want to become a specialist. I'd rather be a GP." At this her mother, Lakshmi, had grown furious. Padma's father, Raghunath, hid his disappointment, as usual.

"You want to be a GP, hah?" Lakshmi demanded. "Not since my mother's time have our people remained mere GPs!"

Sushila winced when Lakshmi slammed a bowl of corn flakes in front of Padma. "Here!" Lakshmi ordered. "Eat!"

"Gee, thanks, Ma."

Although Raghunath frowned at Padma's tone, he remained safe among the columns of his morning paper.

Lakshmi brought Sushila's stewed prunes to the table, then sat and glared at Padma. "None of your back talk to me! Not since my mother's time have we settled for so few credentials. How will you find a good husband with only an MD, hah?"

"I won't," Padma said. "You will." She grinned at Sushila, who responded with a frown of caution. Padma had been born with a monkey grin and it would someday pass to her children.

Now it has, to this first child. He is only a day old in the photo on Sushila's mantel, but she knows that his pout will flower into a grin. Also on the mantel is a letter from Utrecht that reached her office yesterday afternoon. She brought the letter home but did

•

not mention it to Satya. She will, tonight. Perhaps.

She opens the packet and removes both pieces of foil. Then, holding the exposed filters to her nose, she inhales. A newly opened packet of Canadian cigarettes smells like Fig Newton biscuits. She has never told anyone of this, for how would they understand such small pleasures? She removes a cigarette and places the filter between her lips.

She leaves the cigarette unlit.

She never does this if Satya is at home—she does not wish to look like some Indian gangster's gun moll—but he is still at the office. He is reviewing NSERC applications so the researchers in his faculty can produce clean, final drafts. Two more years, and he can retire as dean of science. He will retire without having received a single honorary degree because he preferred administration to research. He prides himself on being a generalist of the old school, not a specialist like her.

He also rarely sits in her two favourite rooms, the only rooms in which she allows herself to smoke: the living room and the kitchen. No good Brahmin would smoke in a kitchen but Sushila does not consider herself orthodox. Satya feels awkward there though he does make his own instant coffee. When entertaining, they use the large family room in the back. This, only when one of her cousins, nieces, or nephews—or one of his own, many relations—comes to Calgary. Satya drives them in his Volvo to Banff and Lake Louise. As for Sushila, she takes visiting colleagues to the faculty club. This saves having to wash the kitchen floor.

The cigarette waggles when she says, "Gun moll, hah?"

Vishnu wags his head. He means, "Maybe yes, maybe no." Then he asks, "Who is there to see?"

Sushila smokes Export A Lights, which come in a gold

coloured packet. She often thinks of switching to a lighter brand, but what does it matter now? A few extra milligrams of tar surely cannot make much difference. She looks at the warning printed on one side in English, on the other in French. This latest packet warns—

Tobacco smoke can harm your children.

La fumée du tabac peut nuire à vos enfants.

She wonders what Padma would say if she knew that Sushila smoked while wrapping the quilt. If anyone interferes, it is Padma—with her repeated warnings about cancer, heart disease. Their conversation on the subject is always brief. Padma asks, "Still smoking, Auntie?" Sushila asks, "Still banging your drum, Monkey?"

She takes out the quilt and ensures that everything is in order. She always does this. Good thing, too, because twice there had been unravelling threads and she had had to endure lengthy exchanges at The Bay. Until children grow old enough to learn how imperfect life can be, they deserve perfection.

The quilt is meant for ages zero to eighteen months and the box promises 5 *Busy Activities! 4 Fun Textures! 4 Happy Sounds!* All of this is true and, though Sushila does not bother verifying the numbers, she does verify the quilt's many features:

—A barn with a padded, crinkling roof.

—Behind the barn's peek-a-boo door, a cow and a mouse.

—A cloth rattle, a removable farmer, secured by Velcro.

She presses the farmer's tummy. She is not sure how long it will be before she can see the boy because neither she nor Satya has a conference upcoming in Vancouver. Next year, perhaps. By then the boy will be crawling and, she is sure, charming everyone. "Our Prince Charming," Padma wrote in the card announcing his birth. She added, "Auntie, Our Prince of Wails."

Padma and her husband have named the boy Ashok. Not good. Not at all good. Sushila does not approve for two reasons. She has told Satya both of these, but she will never tell Padma. First, Ashok is a North Indian name. "South, North," Satya said. "What does it matter? We have lived on this continent so long now, India is India. What does anyone here know about our differences?" Unlike Sushila and her cousins, he never refers to India as *back home*. After forty years in the U.S. and Canada, his India is *over there*.

"It does matter," Sushila said. "Canadians speak of east and west. Americans speak of north and south. They don't like being treated all the same. Why should we?"

"They are not as worldly as you," he said.

Her second objection is far more serious. According to tradition, the first child in any branch of her family is named for the grandmother. Thus, Lakshmi's first grandson should have been given a long, evocative name like Lakshmi Narayan. Not a short one like Ashok. Then again, as Lakshmi said on the phone while hiding her fury—just this once—"Long names are not fashionable here."

This is true. Sushila leans back against a love seat to ease the kink in her neck. Only when she came over in the late 1950s, to the U.S., did she allow people to call her Sheila. Never Sue. But, once she had her Ph.D., she became Dr. Sushila Ramachandra. Those days, before Satya finished his own Ph.D., they received useless mail addressed to Dr. and Mrs. Sushila Ramachandra. Then again, what could one expect of mail-order houses? The mistake annoyed her but Satya found it amusing. "You see?" he said. "Even strangers cannot resist pointing out that I live in your

·

shadow. I am content there."

The filter is beginning to stick to her lips. She removes the cigarette and leaves it, the spongy filter damp, on the rim of her ashtray. Then she finishes her inspection of the quilt:

—A bunny with floppy ears and a red, checked bandana.

—A plastic teething ring shaped like an apple.

—A soft lamb wearing, under its chin, a jingly bell.

Satisfied that there are no loose threads, she refolds the quilt and returns it to the box.

She lights the cigarette at last.

She uses a thin, gold lighter, a gift from Satya. If she must smoke, he wants her lighters to reflect what he calls her elegance. Once, in a blatant hint about her health, he gave her an ivory cigarette holder. She bit through the mouthpiece in a week. Now she inhales deeply before poising the cigarette on the rim of the ashtray. Its cut glass refracts rays from the ceiling light. Rays that cause the border of her sari to glint.

This morning, knowing she would be home all day, she put on her favourite sari. On campus she wears everyday saris. She does so even in her lab, which does not contain the Bunsen burners of her youth. This lab boasts computers, scanners, and colour printers. As for students nowadays, they wear any old thing.

She tilts her head at the child on the front of the box. He must be a boy because his sleeper is blue. The child on the back is a girl. She is also in blue but she wears a frock. She is laughing at the farmer rattle, held by her mother.

Sushila knows Padma will notice that the babies and the mother are white. She, too, will laugh, because these quilts are made in Thailand for North Americans. It is difficult to imagine a Thai child in a crumbling apartment block playing with such a quilt—just as it is difficult to imagine a South Indian child in a bungalow doing the same. But then, Sushila does not send such gifts back home. When each child there is born into the family, she sends a cheque in rupees drawn on her NRI account. She mouths the words *back home*. Even as an Indian bride leaves with her husband, her relations say, "Come home soon." The girl must return to her parents' house to deliver her children, and everyone wants her to have the first child—preferably a boy— soon. But when Sushila's North American nieces and nephews marry, they joke about Auntie buying yet another quilt.

And why not, even if she is a modern woman? Indeed, her womanhood began at twelve even as India became independent. Still, she understands the value of children, though Satya is not concerned about their lack of a son to light their pyres. Or, more likely, to conduct their corpses to a crematorium. Unlike most Brahmins, Satya does not need children to prove that he is doing his duty as a householder. Good thing, too, since they decided not to have children because his younger brother had been born with brain damage. Special needs, they call such children now, in countries that can afford linguistic niceties.

"I have no regrets," she tells Lord Vishnu. She says this often, and she knows he does not believe her. She also tells him it is better that the children from her past life wait to be reborn until after she returns in her next.

Vishnu wags his head noncommittally. He has been toying with the objects he holds: the conch shell, the lotus, the discus, the club. Tired of admiring his reflection, he begins juggling these objects. Given that he has four hands, this is no great trick, but it does help lighten her mood.

She puts down the quilt box and unrolls the craft paper. Then she cuts with the scissors. She knows exactly how much paper to use because she has done this many times, over the years. It has become her own, private tradition. She has bought so many of these quilts that Satya once joked about asking Fisher-Price for a discount. "Ten per cent," he said. "Sushila Discount." He can find humour in anything and why not? He has always been carefree.

She puffs on the cigarette and, though she barely inhales, the nicotine helps her relax. She knows this is not true. It is, indeed, false. She uses nicotine to stimulate her at work and calm her at home although, physiologically, it can only stimulate. She also knows that every intelligent person is stupid about something.

She glances up at the mantel, not at the photo of Baby Ashok but at the letter from Utrecht. She knows what Satya will say: "You should go. He would have wanted you to go."

By *he*, Satya will mean the professor who had influenced her most in Raleigh: Aristid Lindenmayer himself. She had been taking his class in machine theory—the term cybernetics had not yet been coined—and, one day, he had decided to unravel a problem in their textbook. As an open-ended problem, it had no one solution, and yet the exercise had led to a fortuitous discovery. Soon the academy declared Lindenmayer-systems a distinct branch of biomathematics. And, later, he left the U.S. to become director of the University of Utrecht's Theoretical Biology Group.

"Truly a great man," she says.

Nodding with condolence, Vishnu adds, "Truly a good man."

Lindenmayer has been dead for a decade now but his legacy continues—as does, apparently, his influence. For the University of Utrecht has decided to confer upon Sushila an honorary degree. It will be her first. There was a time, long ago, when

·

she craved such recognition. It did not come, and now it means nothing to her. Satya suspects as much. This is why he will no doubt say, "Think of it as honouring your professor. Honouring his legacy."

She quickly wraps the box and secures the brown-paper seams with tape. She miters the corners perfectly. She has always been a perfectionist. How else could she have got this far?

And yet she cannot help wondering whether she has lost the passion of her youth. No, she tells Vishnu. She has not. She is still passionate about her work, especially the progress she has made in the past fifteen years. How many women can use L-systems to grow plants on computer? How many women can create a digital garden that emulates the growth and cyclical nature of a real garden? This includes death, for the plants in every garden face death, just as some of them face rebirth. She grows only perennials.

A cylinder of ash is curving into the ashtray. When she puts the cigarette out, it transfers a last bit of heat to her fingertip. She sucks on this fingertip until it cools.

Then she reaches for her address book. It is also a gift from Satya: a Georgia O'Keeffe address book. On its cover is a painting of a white sails lily. A peace lily. After finding Padma's address, Sushila letters it onto the package. She also letters her return address and, under this in brackets, "Card to Follow." She picks up the package and is surprised by its lightness. She will send it parcel post because there is no rush.

Finished, she pushes the parcel to the far side of the coffee table. On its square, glass top she aligns the address book, the pen, the scissors, the tape, and the craft paper. The roll is smaller than before. Then she reaches for the one, large book that graces the coffee table.

This book is not a collection of photographs by Roloff Benny or of paintings by Mary Pratt. It is *The Algorithmic Beauty of Plants* by Lindenmayer and one of his star collaborators, Przemyslaw Prusinkiewicz. She has never actually read the book but, in odd moments, she glances at the computer-generated photos. She likes their titles: "Pineapples," "Spruce Cones," "The Garden of L." She always looks for her name, in the acknowledgements, to assure herself that the name is still there.

Satisfied, she begins reading halfway down the first page of chapter one:

> The central concept of L-systems is that of rewriting. In general, rewriting is a technique for defining complex objects by successively replacing parts of a simple initial object using a set of *rewriting rules* or *productions*. The classic example of a graphical object defined in terms of rewriting rules is the *snowflake curve*.

Easily bored by prose, she flips to the frontispiece. Here he is, Aristid Lindenmayer, above the years of his birth and death: 1925 to 1989.

She says, "All these numbers, Lord," and sighs.

Only now does she notice that Vishnu has left. His reflection no longer shimmers in the fireplace glass. She decides he has better things to do, someone else to console. That is all right. She can manage. Still, she feels sad, as she always does when looking at this portrait of Lindenmayer. His silver hair is mussed by the wind and much of his face is in shadow. He wears a rumpled shirt. He is examining a purple, flowering plant and, out of focus behind him, lurks a tree or a shrub.

How could she have known he would die so soon after his

•

retirement? In the months following their last meeting, he had co-written and edited many chapters while seriously ill, though she had not learned of the illness until after his death. She likes to remember him as he was in Raleigh—tackling open-ended problems, those with no one solution—but her fondest memory is of that last meeting. Of watching him in front of a select group of students in Prusinkiewicz's seminar room. She had had much to contribute, but she had listened and watched and made notes.

Lindenmayer told the students, "It is one thing to grow plants on computer, in a virtual laboratory. It is quite another to grow animals, because their cells move. Even mutate. Yet I know that every one of you dreams of growing not simply an animal but an entire human being. Well, my young friends, I wish you luck. For the present, however, let us choose an animal."

And so, on a blackboard, he graphed the relationship between the length of a rabbit's tail and the average length of its ears. How everyone laughed—not only because he insisted on referring to it as *our bunny rabbit* but also because, by then, he looked rather like a rabbit himself. He knew this. Like so many good scientists, and Sushila is not sure whether this applies to her, he could explain the most complex of problems simply. Also, unlike her, he was not above poking fun at himself.

The following year, she had been unable to attend his funeral. This is one more reason she knows she must accept the honorary degree. She knows, but she needs to hear it from Satya, and he will tell her what she wants to hear.

She closes the book and marvels at the roses on its cover. Three roses: one orange, two red. She lights another cigarette and leans back against the love seat. Then she waits for Satya to come home. She waits while the afternoon light in the living

•

room fades. There is plenty of time to take the parcel to the post office at the 7 Eleven. They will walk there together after supper and, though the parcel is light, he will insist on carrying it for her. He may not be a scholar, but he is a gentleman. He would have made such a good father.

2

Love and the God of Death

A KING ONCE HAD NO SONS to carry on his line. He prayed to a goddess for eighteen years, and she finally sent him a child. At first he was sad, for he had wanted a son and the child was a girl. Then his wise man said she would grow to be greater than any son. The king named her Savitri, after the goddess who had answered his prayers.

This girl, Savitri, grew to be beautiful and kind. With the wise man to teach her, she also grew learned and clever. She was so beautiful and kind, no one dared ask for her hand. The wise man searched in other kingdoms, but no prince wanted a wife so learned and clever.

One day, Savitri wandered from her father's palace into the forest. Here she found the hut of a hermit. He was blind, and he lived with his son. The young man's name was Satyavan. He spoke like a prince. He was as handsome and loving as she was beautiful and kind. He valued her learning and cleverness. She made him laugh. They barely noticed the sun until it began to set. Then Satyavan said:

A hundred steps taken alone are only a hundred steps.

Seven steps taken with another

Are seven steps taken with a friend.

Savitri ran back to the palace. The bells on her silver anklets

·

134

jingled all the way. She told her father she had found a husband. The wise man told the king that Satyavan had once been a prince. His father had once been a king, but he had gone blind and been overthrown. All seemed well until the wise man looked in the Book of Destiny.

This book belonged to the god of the dead. His name was Yama, and he lived in hell. In this book were marked the names of all mortals. Next to each name was marked the number of years each mortal could spend on earth. Satyavan had only one year to live.

The king told Savitri to choose another young man. She refused. He told her Satyavan's fate but she said she could marry no one else. The wise man advised the king to agree.

And so Satyavan and Savitri circled the wedding fire seven times to become husband and wife. She left the palace and went to live in the hut. She put aside her clothes of silk and wore clothes made of bark. She even put aside her jewellery—all except her silver anklets of bells. This way, when she walked, Satyavan's blind father could hear the bells and know she was close at hand.

The year passed happily. Satyavan gathered firewood. Savitri served his father as if she were his own daughter. At night, Satyavan and Savitri counted the stars.

On the last day of the year, he left the hut before dawn to gather firewood. She begged him to take her with him. He agreed, for she looked sad. It was the first time she had felt sad since their wedding, but she could not tell him why. She could not tell him that this would be his last day on earth.

Satyavan began gathering firewood. Savitri picked fruit. Suddenly, a pain filled his body and he cried out. All he heard, while he lay at the foot of a tree, was the jingling of Savitri's anklets. She cradled his head in her lap and waited while he slid toward death. She waited for the god of the dead.

Soon Yama rode his giant, horned buffalo into sight.

Yama's eyes glinted like copper. His skin was as green as the forest. His robes were as red as the rising sun. With one hand, he carried a mace. From his other hand dangled a noose. He slipped the noose around Satyavan's body and pulled out his soul. Even as the body grew cold, Yama rode south toward hell. All this happened without a sound.

Savitri followed him. She kept her distance. The grass of the forest muffled the jingling of her anklets. So did the water of streams. Only when Yama left the forest did he hear Savitri following him. The ground was rocky and hard, and the bells on her anklets jingled. He stopped his buffalo and turned to face her.

"Your husband is dead," Yama called. "Go back!"

At this she called:

In death as in life,

Satyavan is my husband.

I, Savitri, am his wife.

"I shall only go back," she said, "if you give him back to me."

"I have the power to do that," Yama said, "but I will not." He looked angry. "Tell me why I should even speak with you!"

To this she said:

A hundred steps taken alone are only a hundred steps.

Seven steps taken with another

Are seven steps taken with a friend.

"We have taken many more than that," she said. "We must be friends."

He laughed at her cleverness. "Ask me for a favour," he said.

"Anything but your husband's life."

"My husband's father was overthrown when he went blind," she said. "Please give him back his sight so he may win back his throne."

Yama had expected her to ask the favour for herself. Her lack of selfishness pleased him. "It will be done," he said. "Go back." He flung the noose across his shoulder.

Satyavan's soul swayed while the buffalo continued toward hell. Savitri's anklets jingled while she followed.

Yama stopped for a second time. "Your husband is dead," he called. "Go back!"

At this she called for a second time:

In death as in life,

Satyavan is my husband.

I, Savitri, am his wife.

"I cannot go back," she said, "if you will not give him back to me."

"Your devotion to him pleases me," Yama said. "Ask me for two more favours. Anything but your husband's life."

"My father has no sons to carry on his line," she said. "Please give him many sons."

Once more, Yama had expected her to ask the favour for herself. Once more she had not, and so he was pleased. "It will be done," he said. "What is your last favour?"

"I, too, would like to have sons."

"That, too, will be done."

She thanked him, and he urged his buffalo on, south toward hell. Still, her anklets jingled.

Yama stopped for a third time. "Your husband is dead," he called. "Go back!"

At this she called for a third time:
In death as in life,
Satyavan is my husband.
I, Savitri, am his wife.

"How can I have sons," she asked, "if my husband is dead?"
Enraged, Yama hefted his mace. Then he let it fall onto his shoulder and winced. He began to laugh. He laughed so hard, he had to take great gulps of air. At last he said, "Your husband may live. Go back."

Savitri's anklets jingled while she ran. She ran along the hard, rocky ground. She ran across many streams. She ran along the grass of the forest until she reached Satyavan. She lifted his head and cradled it in her lap while his body grew warm.

He opened his eyes. He mistook her tears of joy for tears of sadness. "How long have I been asleep?" he asked. "And why are you still sad?"

"You have been asleep long enough," she replied. "And I promise I shall never be sad for as long as we live." Hand in hand, they walked through the forest until they reached the hut.

Horses filled the clearing. A hundred warriors knelt before Satyavan's father. He was no longer blind. The warriors had arrived to tell him he was once again a king.

Satyavan was once again a prince. In time he became a king and Savitri became a queen. On the day they were crowned, the wise man gave them his blessing. During the feast that followed, Satyavan often spoke of love and of death. Each time he did this, Savitri and the wise man smiled.

.

3

A Snowflake Curve

IN THOSE FEW MOMENTS before she died, Sushila went in search of
the young man everyone called her husband though the wedding
had yet to take place. They had both agreed to the match, but she
needed to ask him privately, "Are you certain?" She found him
up in the fronds of a palm tree. He was measuring coconuts with
his slide rule, and the silly thing would not remain curved long
enough for him to take accurate readings. "Might as well guess
the sine-cosine of the sun," he said—no, he chuckled—and she
had her reply.

"Satya Narayana," her mother exclaimed. "Such long names
his people have—"

"Musical names," Sushila said, looking up from her chemistry
book.

"—but when they resort to initials, how can I keep them all
straight? The father is RMG, the mother is RLV, but when they
speak of DSV, how am I to know? Is she the elder aunt, or the
younger aunt, or the second cousin once removed whose uncle
was your grandfather's classmate in Benares?"

Sushila could not help. She was memorizing the periodic
table of elements, which unfolded like a Bartholomew map. Only,
the elements would not stay put. What was hydrogen doing next
to zinc? And how could the atomic number of cobalt be twenty-
seven one minute and forty-nine the next? And, oh, how much

•

progress Madame Curie could have made had she owned a juicer. No more squeezing a thousand lemons by hand simply to find the new element that had ruined the X-rays in her jewellery box.

"Still," Sushila's mother went on, as she always went on. "You must never refer to your husband by name when you speak of him to someone else. No good Hindu wife does this, lest she bring the evil eye upon him. Or some such thing. I knew, once."

"Even in America?" Sushila asked.

"I do not know about Americans," her mother replied. "You must tell me all about their peculiar customs when you write, which you will do—once every month—using only this fountain pen that I am gifting to you. And this peacock coloured ink."

Goddess Lakshmi agreed. "Regular as clockwork," she said. This, while she rode an escalator down to the garden from a Lockheed Constellation. Its propellers were ceiling fans; its contrails braided into cotton candy as blue as Vishnu's skin. The goddess stroked the tail of her peacock, which decided it would rather be a brass firescreen. Only, who would light a fire in Raleigh on the Fourth of July?

"They take marshmallows and do what!" Sushila asked. While Satya laughed. Now, though, she knew when he was joking and, even better, the children were at last in school.

She had named the girl Bhagirathi, the boy Lakshmana; yet everyone called them Rita and Luke. Satya claimed that the change would help them fit in. "No," she insisted. "They have lost something, however intangible. Have you seen my sewing needle case? That ivory one from Hyderabad with the inlaid eyes."

To which Satya wagged his head: maybe yes, maybe no. Maybe nonlinear control systems, why not? Carrying a full load left her little time for research although, once, she had dreamt of unifying all the many, partial theories of nonlinear control systems into a practical, general theory. But she would never make a significant contribution to her field, not after having stayed home for so long. For the children's sake. Oh, for goodness sake, what was this plastic band doing on her wrist where her bangles should be? The white gold bangles her mother had worn, one on each of her four goddess-like wrists, iron hard from squeezing a thousand lemons a day—no, limes—while she kept on calling, "Sushila? Where are you, Monkey? All these dishes to prepare, and still the chutney is not done!"

And how could Sushila play the *veena* while floating on her back like this? Not even Goddess Saraswati could pluck these strings unless she sat cross-legged on the floor, jasmine and rose perfuming the air, an audience that came and went—in focus one minute, cotton candy blurred the next.

Like Satya's voice, humming with a constellation of bees when he spoke to Rita, Daddy's little girl, who could do no wrong. Not like Luke—silly boy—refusing to follow his sister into graduate school like that. Not nearly as ambitious as one would expect of the son of educated people. Wanting to be a woodworker, of all things, even as he tried to follow in the footsteps of Satya's father by joining the civil service. True, Satya was touched by this latter, but he could never say so to the boy, and now it might be too late.

Later in the dining room than in the living room, even later in the kitchen, for the time zones changed from room to room in this posh Calgary house: the living room on eastern time, the dining room on central time, the kitchen on mountain time. But the worst of it was—how could she serve the food piping hot, as every proper hostess should, when the guests at her teakwood table were an hour ahead of her stove?

•

That was her mother's job every morning, and not one she could trust to the servants: she rose before dawn, lit the fire, made her husband his morning coffee, set two Gluco biscuits on a plate, and only then woke him. Even as Sushila drifted like sandalwood incense through the house. She found him in his study, where the clocks were kept on Greenwich time. Where a brass orrery from Florence twirled its planets around their moons and the sun around the earth. That sine-cosine sun whose face she could not read, not even with her father's ivory slide rule.

And how precise Rita was, how accurate her taking of measurements. How lucid her reports. Imagine: assistant director of an NMR facility at twenty-nine. Nuclear magnetic resonance. Even the term had resonance. Far more than nonlinear control systems—what a mouthful that was. But nothing could resonate like the simplest of words and phrases. Take daughter, take wife, take mother of two fine children.

"A few more years," Luke said, "and you might be a grandmother, too. Maybe even sooner." He was smiling like an imp while he nodded at his masterpiece: a row of cabinets in honey coloured oak, their doors of bevelled glass.

And imagine this: a man of twenty-seven as eager as a boy while Sushila unwrapped the tissue paper that protected her collection of boxes. Though she had never meant to start a collection, not when she had bought this first one as a souvenir of her Agra honeymoon. The box was made of greenish stone that was soft enough to be carved, in a trellis pattern, through all four sides. So soft, if she kept it on the windowsill its removable lid would melt in the sun. Unless she watered it every day to keep the multicoloured ovals, inlaid to form grapes, shiny and plump.

·

The box looked vaguely Italianate, and why not? She had bought it in a craft emporium close to Taj Mahal and, from up close, the inlaid walls of the Taj also looked Italianate.

So the old woman had said even as she had handed Sushila the box and given her strict instructions for its care. The blind old woman who knew when the moon was full because she could hear it singing to young brides. Singing, "Come home soon."

"We shall see," Sushila told Luke. "There is no one special yet in your sister's life." Except perhaps this new fellow: a biogeologist, good family, Ashok by name. And though Rita, like her brother, had been born on this continent, she felt duty bound as the elder to marry first. "Good, good," Sushila said.

"Pardon?" Luke asked. He was folding tissue paper into star maps. Here shone Cassiopeia, there Andromeda.

"You are hearing things again, son." But even as she spoke— even as she heard herself speak—she sensed that something was wrong. It was the chutney. The coriander chutney looked crimson; the pomegranate chutney was a forest green.

So that was it: the gods were toying with the blind old woman. She could see the moon at last but could not hear it sing. And where had the goddesses gone? Lakshmi with her peacock. Saraswati with her *veena*. Where the palm trees and limes? The constellations of bees. The aroma of jasmine and rose. Worse— everything seemed clear now, the focus too sharp, and Sushila felt uneasy. But Luke might shrug if she asked why and how, so she watched him and listened, all the while hoping he could show her the way. Back to where she felt most at home: on the stone floor of her mother's kitchen; in the teakwood chairs of her father's study; among the tamarind and mango, the almond and marigold in the gardens of their Mysore house.

•

"Will it bother you if I don't get a permanent job?" Luke asked.

"Certainly not, and Nora will love you just the same."

Yes, Sushila was convinced that Nora adored Luke as much as he adored her. And her parents treated him like a son. Best of all, Satya approved of her. He once commented, "If the boy can't marry an Indian girl, better he should marry a Jew. They are much like us. They live the questioning life—"

"And," Sushila added, "they know what it is to keep moving."

He laughed at this, his eyes dancing at the thought of Nora as his daughter-in-law. It was a pity they had not seen her for some months now. After finishing her master's, she had taken a short-term contract in Edmonton. Luke spent his weekends there, in her small flat, but Nora claimed that she could not spare the time to visit this house. Which did not sound at all like her.

"Let us take a break," Sushila said. "Decaffeinated is fine?" Without waiting for Luke's nod, she walked from the living room into the foyer, past the formal dining room, and entered the kitchen. Here, the clock on the coffee maker was two hours behind the clock on the living room mantel. This was as it should be, and it dispelled her earlier unease. Instead of reaching for the glass carafe, she filled a hibiscus with water and took it into the sun porch. Here it was Pacific time, three hours behind the living room, and even as she sat in her usual spot—facing lilacs along a fence made of wedding saris—the front doorbell rang.

"I'll get it," Luke called. She heard him open the door and say, "Hul-lo," in his father's cultured voice. Then she heard nothing except the wind in the lilacs until she heard him in the kitchen. "She's in back," he said. "Hang on a sec. There." His voice was tender, and Sushila knew there was only one person in the world besides herself to whom he spoke so tenderly.

"Is that you, Nora?" Sushila called.

"Long time, Ma," Nora said.

"Come," Sushila called. "My wedding saris are in bloom."

She was tucking a strand of hair behind her ear when Nora entered the sun porch. Luke was close behind her. And not until Nora sat in Luke's usual spot did Sushila realize Nora was holding a bundle. She propped the higher end of the bundle against her upper arm and folded back a corner of the yellow flannel blanket. Luke stood near a hanging basket of plush toys. His hands were in his trouser pockets, he was rocking to and fro, and he was beaming.

Sushila asked, "What is all this?" Excitement and dread caused her mouth to go dry, so she took another sip of water.

"We wanted to surprise you," Luke said. "And Pa." Then he said to Nora, "You tell her."

"Tell me what?" Sushila asked, though the answer was forming in her mind. These two monkeys; so this was why Nora had not come to the house in all these months.

"It's true I've been in Edmonton," she said, "but I wasn't just working on a contract." Her tentative smile became radiant. She turned the bundle so that Sushila could see the baby's face. "We're calling him David Satya Narayana. Mom and Dad have known all along, but we made them swear not to tell."

Sushila could believe neither her eyes nor her ears, not even after Luke said, "It's true, Ma. Your very first grandchild. David Satya Narayana Goldblum. That a mouthful or what?"

Although Sushila wanted to hold the child, Nora still cradled him. He looked all of a week old. He looked just like Luke. Even as Nora said, "I think David's good for short," Sushila began to

·

laugh. She was so touched by their joy, she did not ask if they had married. She clapped, then left her hands together. She raised her hands to her chin. She could not wait to see the look on Satya's face when he came home; could not wait to watch him struck dumb when he learned of his grandchild. What she would not give to see him here this instant. See him baffled, for once. Watch him appraise their son in this new light—in the spill of moonlight that dazzled her even as it promised, "Home."

•

Acknowledgements

I WROTE AND REVISED this book between late 1977 and early 2003. The following agencies provided me with generous financial support: The Canada Council for the Arts, the Department of Canadian Heritage, the Saskatchewan Arts Board, the City of Regina Arts Commission, and Warren Wilson College. I also held posts as a writer in residence that were supported by The Canada Council for the Arts, The University of Calgary's Markin-Flanagan Distinguished Writers Programme, the Scottish Arts Council, the Department of English at the University of Alberta, the Regina Public Library, the Department of English at McMaster University, and the Yukon Public Libraries.

Portions of this book have been previously published. "Amar's Gift" appeared in a special international fiction issue, edited by David Albahari, of *Descant* magazine. And "Sushila Is at Home" appeared in *04 Best Canadian Stories,* edited by Douglas Glover. My thanks go to both of these editors. And I wrote "Rainbow Knights" for my cousin, Krishna Arun Burra.

Finally, thanks go to my ex-wife, Shelley Sopher, for her patience and insights while I wrote and revised this book during the many years of our marriage.

·

VEN BEGAMUDRÉ

VEN BEGAMUDRÉ WAS BORN in South India and came to Canada when he was six. He has an honours degree in Public Administration from Carleton University and a Master of Fine Arts in Creative Writing from Warren Wilson College. He has held numerous residencies, including the Canada-Scotland Exchange Writer in Residence. His work has appeared in Canada, the United States, the Netherlands, and Scotland. He has won a number of awards including the 2018 Regina Public Library Saskatchewan Book of the Year Award for *Extended Families: A Memoir of India*. *The Teller from the Tale* is his tenth book. Ven lives in Regina, Saskatchewan.